3

GOOD GOSSIP

GOOD Gossip

JACQUELINE CAREY

RANDOM HOUSE

NEW YORK

Portions of this work were originally published
in *The New Yorker* and *Wigwag*.

Library of Congress Cataloging-in-Publication Data

Carey, Jacqueline.
Good gossip / Jacqueline Carey.
p.   cm.
ISBN 0-394-57638-1
I. Title.
PS3553.A66855G66   1992
813'.54—dc20   91-52683

Manufactured in the United States of America
2 4 6 8 9 7 5 3
First Edition
Text set in Weiss
Book design by Jo Anne Metsch

To Sandy

CONTENTS

GOOD GOSSIP

GOOD GOSSIP

*veryone was surprised when Dee Kilmartin first passed around the news that Susannah was going to marry Harry Tierney. The rhyme "marry Harry" became kind of a joke the spring before the wedding. If you got yourself into a hole telling a story—if no one laughed at the end, and you had to keep going—you could always work your way around somehow to an "I could always marry Harry" and gratifying hilarity.

Not that Harry Tierney was laughable in himself. He was a fellow who tried awfully hard. He was a senior associate at a Wall Street law firm, and he worked, say, eighty hours a week. Doing what, no one knew, although he must have told Susannah. He was the sort of man who turned evil fast on a soap opera, because what audience could stand such unrelenting earnestness day after day? But despite his job he was just right to sit next

3

to at dinner, which I did once. It was the only time I'd actually talked to him before the engagement. He had a way of wrinkling his brow while listening that was most flattering. He wasn't embarrassing (wasn't, you know, too much of a toady), the way we all imagined those people to be. Nor was he hideous, although his face was perhaps a trifle pudgy, and his body a bit, mmm, unformed.

It's just that Susannah had complained about him for at least a year before the announcement of their engagement. At one particularly drunken party downtown at Dee Kilmartin's, Susannah had fallen into my lap and cried, "Oh, Rosemary. He's so *boring*, he's so *boring*. Just *look* at him. Oh, God, *everything* is so *boring*." Unfortunately, she was close to being right, and not just about Harry Tierney. It was getting hard to sort out the parties: all the regulars just walked through their roles, and the guest stars were looking entirely too familiar. For me, turning thirty was too much like hitting the end of the season, when reruns began. Susannah tumbling on me was different enough that I didn't mind her crumpling my new second-hand skirt, although it meant an extra trip to the hateful dry cleaners on Broadway.

The biggest break in routine, however, was the impending marriage itself, which completely overshadowed any of Susannah's past theatrics. Our first theory—formed quite early, back in February, barely a week after the announcement—was that she was going to marry for money. Susannah may have had a harder time starting out than the rest of us. According to Dee, she first came

to town to become an actress. Since I'd never heard of
Susannah going to plays or otherwise showing an interest in drama, this plan must have expressed some vague
need rather than true professional intent. Whichever, it
didn't work out, and I don't know what she did for
money then, or later, when she was back in school,
studying design. She got free meals by hanging around
certain hotel bars—or so she claimed. For a while, she
lived out of a suitcase in the supply room of a health
club. That much I know, because she took me over there
one day. The suitcase was large and pale blue; her parents had given it to her for her high school graduation.
"Little did they imagine," she said as she snapped open
the clasps and pulled out a pink watch cap.

But that was a long time ago. Now, at a time when
most people we knew were quitting their jobs in a panic
of boredom, she'd just landed a new one with a design
firm, and she was making more money than most of us
were. Besides which, she had a nice cheap sublet on East
Tenth Street, so she didn't need Harry Tierney's high-
rent floor-through in Chelsea.

Actually, we lit on the money theory because we
found it thrilling. "Just like a Balzac novel," said Cole at
the Horse Bar near Liz Quirk's, and Liz and Joey Bertrand and I silently wondered at the sacrifice Susannah
had made for so artistic an end. Even Liz, who had once
fantasized about marriage to a famous basketball player,
saying, "The only color I care about is green," was in awe
of the reality.

Joey was the first to talk sense: "But didn't she just get a job?"

"That's true," I said. "Last time I saw her, she was talking about all the things she was going to spend her salary on."

"She wouldn't marry for money now," said Joey. "Maybe in six months, when she's gotten used to those paychecks, and she's found out what she can't buy. . . ." So we got off on a tangent about how nowadays no one could live on money that at one time would have seemed astronomical, and we got so bored we soon found ourselves watching the color TV over the bar instead of talking.

I'd known these three people so long (Cole and Joey I met in college; Liz I met before my first year in New York was up), and each of us had seen the others in so many combinations that a certain blending had gone on, and I found it difficult to credit any of them with pasts or· jobs very different from my own. As a result, many of our stories were as disembodied yet as familiar as plots of TV shows, so the transition from talking to watching was not an abrupt one.

Susannah I knew less well. I'd met her only a few years before, through Dee Kilmartin, who gives a lot of parties and so knows far too many people to know anyone in quite the way normal people do, and everyone at the Horse Bar that night knew Susannah through me. That's quite a distance, friend of a friend, even if everyone's been to the same parties. I didn't see her for several weeks after I first heard the news, but I occasionally saw someone who would refer archly to the "business deal" maturing in June, or someone who wouldn't let go of that "marry Harry" singsong. The whole thing had gotten a little silly by the time Cole and I met Susannah in the bar by the police station, and we'd decided we weren't going to talk about it.

She was late, and Cole and I had had time for a drink before she arrived, so we were able to make a good show of our congratulations when she walked in. Before responding, she took off her coat. It was a bit heavy for March, but worth any discomfort: long and cut wide, made of thick black karakul. She had to feel around for the buttonholes, and then it took a lot of careful tugging to free the buttons, which were large with crescent indentations. "I cannot bear to discuss it," she said finally, and as she sighed the voluminous coat fell over the back of the stool, nearly tipping it over. She sank into the folds, newly slender. "I have discussed it and discussed it, and if I have to discuss it again I will barf."

That's the way she talks. If you weren't as fond of her as I was, or if she hadn't quite so many parts comparable to poetic objects, you might say she had a vulgar streak. When she shook out her long black hair, the slow curls played off each other like plaster patterns in a bedroom ceiling. To think of all this ensnared by Harry Tierney— well, it was hard.

"I went to the butcher around the corner yesterday," she said, "and the most incredible lassitude overtook me as soon as I opened the door. I could barely move my legs, like in one of those terrible dreams. I just stood there while everyone else pushed forward to get their boring cuts of meat. I could have been in there an hour —I don't know, because my brain wasn't working, either. I couldn't stop thinking about all the times I've bought food, and all the times I was going to buy food. All those millions of pieces of meat and all those millions of pieces of bread and all those millions of pieces of lettuce. It's enough to make you sick."

"I suppose we'll have to drink our dinner," said Cole, but his face was glum. We all looked at the table next to ours, where hideous laughter was swelling.

I said, "We're not really going to have such a terrifically good time tonight, are we?"

So once again we broke up early. Susannah headed uptown, and Cole and I were left on a corner beside an empty basketball court crisscrossed with shadows from the chain-link fence. "Depression stalks even the least likely of us," said Cole.

"It gets around."

"Money does not seem to be on her mind."

"No."

"You don't think she's getting married out of boredom, do you?"

"Marry *Harry Tierney* out of boredom?"

"I suppose not."

*   *   *

The inversion of flourish and line in left-handedness has always had a special charm for me. Left-handed Susannah turns the face of her watch onto the inside of her right wrist, for instance; telling the time requires only the subtlest falling back of the fingers instead of the unnatural lifting and crooking of the elbow other people go through. Yet to write the simplest grocery list she snakes her hand around three sides of a piece of paper.

Since she'd moved in, her sublet had acquired a similar, odd delicacy. Furniture lent to friends of the real tenant had never been replaced, powder puffs ballooned in corners, glasses were all shot size. In the kitchen, underneath the marble slab holding makeup in Mona Lisa tomato cans, was a row of vodka bottles. Cole was lifting them one at a time and gauging their contents. Susannah, in a pink slip, picked a record off the stereo and ran it over her thigh to remove the dust. She was begging for news about people who would be at that night's party: "I've been so out of it, I don't know what's going on, and you guys always know the good gossip."

Cole, busy pouring vodka, said, "Let me think . . ."

I thought of quite a good story about Dee Kilmartin, but then Susannah said, "I'll tell you what I've been doing. Meeting his family, for one thing."

"Harry's, you mean."

"It was absolutely exhausting. Harry is such a—well, a serious type, you know. . . ."

"So I hear. I've never talked to him," said Cole.

Susannah dismissed this with a twist of her hand. "It

didn't prepare me for his family, but I should have known; he never said anything about them except how much fun they were, what a good time they have. The fact is, they're a laugh-track family. 'Hey, have a beer, chortle, chortle.' 'Don't mind if I do, chortle, chortle.' No matter what anyone said, everyone laughed. And one sister kept up a quiet *ha-ha-ha, ha-ha-ha* all the time, to sort of keep her motor running. They made Harry look so mercifully sane. I smiled so much I thought my face would crack. It was infuriating, but I had to be polite about it, so I started *agreeing* with them. I said, 'Yes, that is funny, isn't it?' or 'How amusing. Almost as good as a dead-baby joke.' "

"Did they catch on?"

"Who knows? They all laughed, of course." Susannah pointed at a glass of vodka, which I handed to her. "The parents were the same, only milder. The mother said about me to Harry, 'Such a nice, quiet girl.' "

"Ah, they're in for a shock," said Cole gallantly.

"At least you can see why Harry got so serious," I said. "It's an admirable reaction in a way."

"I don't think Harry knows how serious he is," said Susannah. "They all laughed at everything he said, too."

No one I know goes to parties alone. I suppose you might meet the man of your dreams, but with whom would you discuss him afterward? There is nothing sweeter than comparing notes, especially with Susannah. Since Dee Kilmartin knows so many people, she tends to have a single line about even those closest to her. About

Susannah she says, "She never looks back." In fact, Susannah looks back all the time, but never with regret. Half of most people's stories are lost, because they're too embarrassed to tell them. Nothing was too awful for Susannah to admit to, even boast about, and in detail. You could always count on an unexpurgated, if somewhat fanciful, version of the night.

To prepare for a party together is almost as much fun, though. As Susannah dressed (much snapping and ironing, painting and powdering, then one last smooth silken tug), I speculated on some newly minted animosities and what form they would take that night. Cole, who smokes only on special occasions, lit three cigarettes, one after another. Susannah pirouetted in front of a mirror with the glass of vodka, smiling. Her dissatisfaction didn't start until we left the apartment. "The earrings are all wrong," she said as she turned the key on the police lock.

"Why?" I asked. At each ear three triangles fanned out.

"They're too sixties for this dress." That was on the first landing.

"I like the contrast."

"Yes. . . . Still, maybe the idea is too subtle for these people." That was halfway down, and involved a slight hanging back.

"You look fine."

"They might think I don't know what I'm doing."

By the time we'd descended the five flights of narrow stairs to the street, she'd decided to change the earrings.

Cole and I sat on the stoop in the fine spring air, and as soon as the door shut behind us he said, "You notice how she kind of glows?"

"Sort of. I bet she's happy."

"I bet she's pregnant. There's your answer."

"She is not pregnant, and I wish you would return to this century."

"It's true that the sort of nobility involved was far more common in the nineteenth century. You see, Harry Tierney is *not the father.*"

"And why isn't she getting an abortion?"

"Sentiment."

"That is the silliest thing I ever heard."

Cole was unperturbed. "So?"

"And what do you know about sentiment, anyway?" I asked.

He was trying to rub a scuff from his shoe. "Just what I learned from you," he said.

The party that night was the best one we'd been to in ages.

A few days after I received an invitation to the wedding, I told Cole, since that is not the sort of thing I keep from him. He hadn't gotten one—not unexpectedly, since he and Susannah didn't know each other apart from me—so I rented a car with Dee Kilmartin. The wedding was in a church, in one of those Long Island towns with one nestling green hollow per house. Susannah had a white train a dozen pews long (I counted). Accompanying her

were Harry's two sisters, Holly and Hester, each carrying a fistful of yellow tulips. I saw no sign of undue
mirth, or any mirth at all. It was beautiful and quick, and
it did not prepare me for what came later.

The reception was held in a country club on Long
Island Sound. You could see the tiny light-colored artifi-
cial beach and the smart white rows of docked boats
from the table where Dee Kilmartin and I sat, flanked by
a couple of Susannah's friends from high school. We
were on a kind of porch attached to the room with the
bar. The shutters that had formed the outside wall had
been rolled up, and the air was all crisp, cool breezes
sweet enough to break your heart. Dee was talking to
the friend on her side, and I was wondering what to say.
I had outgrown my snide teenage habit of asking at the
reception, "How long do you think it will last?," but I
didn't know what should replace it. I hadn't been to a
wedding for ten years—since the summer all my older
cousins tied the knot, one, two, three, the way light
bulbs burn out one right after another. To be honest, this
wedding overwhelmed me; it was so much how things
were supposed to be and so little like Susannah throwing
herself on my lap.

The high school friend on my side made some small
effort, but whatever she said bored her so much she
didn't bother to enunciate. I was about to ask her to
repeat herself when Susannah appeared, minus her train
and headpiece but still in her white dress. She sat on the

table between us, crossed her legs, and asked, "So how was I?"

Wind stirring the boats beyond us drove metal against metal; cloth snapped; inside, a horn began to play. I changed my mind—this would be fun. Dee leaned over me and began to make remarks. Susannah drained what was left of my drink and pointed to the pastel choker worn by the gal next to her. "Is that the kind of necklace you can eat?" she asked. Even Dee Kilmartin laughed, and she hates to be interrupted.

Susannah was sitting with her shoulders slightly hunched so that she could comfortably grasp the edge of the table, her skirt hiked up, her legs still crossed, the top one swinging freely. Because there was a shimmer in the thick white stuff of her wedding dress, her slightest movement was embellished with grace notes. So it was all the more noticeable when in a few minutes she quieted down, her eyes focused on the arched doorway. We all looked, too, and watched Harry Tierney walk toward us.

There's never enough room in tuxedo pants for a normal guy's calves, so the fabric bunches up over them: the look is manly but silly, like callused hands sticking out beneath French cuffs. The line was particularly bad on Harry Tierney, and I felt a stab of affection for him.

He was neither flattered nor disconcerted by the attention—no more aware of Susannah's change than he'd be if his watch had stopped. Several days later, when I was talking with Cole and Joey and an unnaturally quiet new friend of Joey's named Fern, I said, "Of course that sudden stillness could have been love. It would be a bore —I expect more operatic emotions out of her—but it's possible, in which case no further explanations are necessary," but I could count on Cole to disagree: "No one's saying she doesn't love him; we're not looking for crude explanations here—we're looking for something more subtle. The question is, Why does she love him in a way that makes her want to marry him? Given the history, I mean."

At the time, though, Susannah's sudden quiet looked a lot more like annoyance than love. When Harry took her away to begin the dancing, I asked the friend near me, "Do you know him at all?"

Dee said, "She's made a good choice. So different from the losers she used to go out with. Remember the guy who left her stranded in Brazil?"

"Don't forget the one who almost killed her," said the woman beside her.

The fourth at the table said, "What?"

Dee said, "This is one of those secrets you keep until you realize that everyone else in the world knows it, and then you feel like a jerk."

"For some reason I always thought that story was apocryphal," I said.

"You didn't know her back then."

"Who was it? Someone I know?" asked the friend beside me.

"Some artist," said the other friend.

"He was an extremely bad sculptor," Dee amended. "That part is hardly worth mentioning. He tried to smother her with a pillow, in bed."

"Well, it was a long time ago. Besides, he was tripping. I don't think that really counts."

"I certainly don't know in what sense it doesn't count," said Dee.

The two high school friends and Dee and I spent most of the evening outside on the veranda. Good-looking waiters brought us drinks and little triangular sandwiches and clams and shrimp. The other table out there was usually empty, and except when the setting sun shot a pure red arrow across the sound, the few people who wandered out were soon driven elsewhere by the chill in the air. I stayed for the camaraderie. When one guest too many had commented on the sunset, for instance, the friend next to me gave me a look under lowered brows and said, "Wearing a dress like that, and she's still interested in postcards." Dee, who overheard, nodded. I didn't know what was meant about the dress (Was it particularly daring or costly?—to me it just looked red and long), but I liked the implication of a shared knowledge. Also, the main hall was not inviting: relatives can be depressing even when they're not your own. And lawyers can be worse. But eventually we had to go back in for toasts. As we found purses and matches, a waiter pulled at a metal bar and the shutters rolled down behind us.

Harry's brother was finishing his speech when we entered. Glasses bobbed up and down through the crowd. Some Tierneys giggled. Then a young man in a white suit lifted his glass and said, "When I first saw Susannah, I thought she was the world's greatest catch."

A contortion of the crowd pushed me against Dee, who whispered, "That was at the party she went to wearing only a fishnet body stocking and a corsage."

"Congratulations to you both," the toast continued.

"She doesn't seem to have caught the double meaning," I whispered back.

"Why? What would she do? Blush? Come on, she loves it."

Susannah did look great, up by the cake. She was too unpredictable to be graceful, but she had a wonderful sense of drama. Right now, the way she gazed out over the crowd as she acknowledged acclaim made Harry Tierney look like the politician's spouse.

Acting the politician was beyond her, however. No more than ten minutes later, when she dragged Harry's brother over to us, she said, "You really have got to hear this; it's unbelievable."

"Hear what?" he said. And sure enough, there it was— just the faintest *ha-ha-ha, ha-ha-ha,* as his words trailed off.

Polite as always, Dee Kilmartin said of Susannah, "Doesn't she look great?" and Harry's brother replied, "All brides are beautiful, because it's the happiest day of their lives." The laugh was becoming better defined.

Harry came up and bent over Susannah's ear.

"Just a minute," she said, stepping away from him. Harry touched her shoulder, then thought better of it and bent again over her ear.

"Just a minute," she said. This time she jiggled the arm between them, as if to shake him off.

When he spoke the next time, the words were distinct: "But the car's waiting."

"Oh, do let me be for just a minute," she said. And then she said loudly, proclaimed really, "I'll tell you the happiest time of my life. It was when I was in Amsterdam. The American Field Service had sent me. Yes, I was an AFS student—can you believe it? I'd been sent to Germany, but I couldn't stand it. The girl in the family I was supposed to live with was two years younger than I was, and she followed me everywhere. I even caught her pretending to read my diary, though she couldn't understand a word of English. So I hitchhiked to Holland. I called my mother, and she sighed and said, 'Just don't tell your father.' I had a great time. Every week I'd go on the tour at the brewery around the corner and meet another guy. I started off with Americans, but I got to like the Dutch better. When I went back to the States, everyone smirked and said, 'So how were the *Low* Countries?' But my father didn't find out for years."

Harry's brother's laughter continued unabated, but Harry said, "Everyone's already heard that story." This was rude but not unjustified. I had heard it, oh, maybe a dozen times. She always got a kick out of "*Low* Countries." I looked at shoes: Dee was wearing short, square-heeled pumps; next to those were some narrower, cream-colored sling-backs.

"At least it's a good story," said Susannah. I let my eyes rise a bit higher. The line of her skirt, which followed her hips and thighs and then flared out below her knees, made her look a little like a folded umbrella.

"Yes, yes, of course," said Harry Tierney. I couldn't keep my eyes on him long. His face wasn't exactly red, but it had that bright, hot aura that made you wish you were watching something prerecorded and heavily rehearsed. It would have been easier if he'd been better-looking. Or if he hadn't been wearing that tux.

"You find it amusing, don't you?" Susannah said to the brother, whose motor faltered. "I can tell."

When I described this to Cole and Joey and Joey's friend Fern, Joey asked if she'd been very drunk, and I said, "It's hard to tell with her, but I don't think she had the chance to drink much."

Fern, who can be as spooky as an underground cave, nodded. "This person wants stability but despises it at the same time."

"Is that why she married Harry, do you think?" I asked Cole.

"Not good enough," he said. "Who *doesn't* fit that description?"

Fern said, "I'll ask my cousin—she's a therapist."

As soon as "marry Harry" disappeared from our vocabulary, Susannah became known to people who hadn't even met her as the bride who wouldn't leave on her honeymoon.

I don't know many married people my own age. In fact, I'd say I know only one other couple at all well, and they live in Seattle. The wife and I were roommates in college freshman year, so they've visited a couple of times. Maybe it was the city that brought this out, but I swear those two could have been stuck together with Krazy Glue. They even went to the bathroom together—a practice I found disgusting. Ordinarily, I suppose, it wouldn't bother me, but this was *my* bathroom, which is three feet by four feet, including tub. I mean, where did the other person stand?

So I don't have any experience with what I'd consider normal husbands and wives, but Susannah's marriage struck me as excessively different. Despite her pointed lingering at the reception, which couldn't have gone on for more than half an hour, Susannah came back from her honeymoon as if she'd just had a great weekend fling: she was tanned, happy, rested. Also, Harry Tierney never really surfaced again. Before the wedding, Susannah had usually been busy with some arcane chore (invitations, caterers), but now she was free once more, and she showed up at parties without him, or met people for drinks for nights on end. I'm not complaining; I didn't relish the idea of trying to swap stories with Harry Tierney, but still I thought it was odd.

One night, about two months after the wedding, my

phone rang. I had been dreaming that I was going from room to room looking for clues to something, when the whole place shrank to a mere dollhouse, and I was looking in at a lot of buzzing, mechanical men—until I was completely awake, and the buzzing turned into ringing. It was two o'clock in the morning.

I figured it was someone just out of a dinner, drunk, with a great piece of gossip. I try to be gracious about this, since I used to do it myself, but I thought, Two o'clock on a Tuesday night, the worst night of the week —this had better involve incarceration at the very least.

It was Harry, apologetic, asking for Susannah. When I told him she wasn't with me, he asked, "Didn't you have dinner together? When did she leave?"

"Oh, she's with a bunch of people," I said. This was probably not untrue, although I couldn't be sure; I hadn't seen her in over a week. "Really, I wouldn't worry. She probably can't find a cab."

Harry said good-bye as if he'd been clubbed.

I tried to reach Susannah the next day at work, but she was off looking at some samples of air ducts, so I left a message for her to call. She didn't. When I finally got her the following day, I shouted. "I don't want to know what you were doing," I said. "If you wouldn't even tell me, it's got to be pretty bad. But next time you use me as a cover like that, at least give me some kind of warning."

Susannah was so quiet and meek in response I didn't know what was going on, so I called Cole and told him about it, and he said Dee Kilmartin had told him that the

same thing had happened to Dotty Coombs, who hadn't
seen Susannah in months.

"What a criminal she's turned out to be," I sighed.

"She's not doing anything she didn't use to do."

"Except now she's married."

"Except now she's married," he repeated. "Harry Tierney must have put a certain kick back into her life.
Maybe that's it. It's so much easier to be bad when you've
got a husband. You don't have to stay out nearly so late."

It was true that Susannah was looking better than ever.
She had had her hair cellophaned, and the glow that
Cole had remarked on got more pronounced. There was
no more talk from her about how buying food made her
sick. Susannah had always excited comment, but as the
weeks passed, it got ridiculous, even though I could see
why heads turned. Once, I actually heard an otherwise
unimpressible young man say, "So that's Susannah Tierney." Worse, Liz Quirk's sister from Maine, who didn't
know that I knew Susannah, pointed her out to me as she
walked into a restaurant one night.

Six months after the wedding, at one of Dee Kilmartin's
parties, Susannah sailed by Liz Quirk and me saying,
"Talking about me behind my back again?"

I was startled, partly because we hadn't been, and
partly because of the brief, happy picture she made: like
a satisfied crocodile in a cartoon—all abashed grin.

"She's looking good," said Liz.

I nodded.

"Could it be Harry?" Liz was still gazing off in the direction in which Susannah had disappeared. "I never met the fellow, but I always wondered why *he* married *her*, rather than vice versa."

I swirled the ice cubes in my glass impatiently. This was a lie; Liz had used "marry Harry" as often as anyone else. "Brains, beauty, charm," I said.

"Conceding all that. There must be tons of women in New York you could say the same of."

"That would have Harry?"

"He doesn't sound like such a bad sort." Revisionism has set in already, I thought.

Dee, who had joined us at some point, said, "He's got the job, she's got the past—it's a common combination."

Liz pursed her lips. "It sounds to me like she's got the present; isn't that the problem?"

We were interrupted again, so I didn't get a chance to ask Liz if she was referring to anything new. The question would have interested me more if I hadn't been quite so taken with Susannah's grin and the startling happiness it revealed.

The next day I tried to explain this to Cole and Dee and, simply because they were with us, two friends of hers who worked in a museum. "Isn't she the one who went on a separate honeymoon from her husband?" asked one of the friends.

"No, no," said Dee, and I said, "Not exactly." We were seated somewhat awkwardly in a Japanese restaurant. We were the only customers, but each table was built for four, so the fifth person, Cole, stuck out into the aisle. A gas heater breathed heavily beside us.

Without waiting for me to go on, Cole said that Joey told him he'd run into Susannah in the street. "He said she was with some extremely vulpine young man."

"Ah." I put my chopsticks down and folded my hands.

"He was laughing."

"Oh, that's different." I picked up the chopsticks. "A Tierney, no doubt."

"No doubt."

"Although I would hardly characterize the Tierney look as vulpine."

"But you see, it doesn't matter. Automatically he's interesting—to you, to me, to everyone—because he's not the husband."

I thought this over as Dee started to explain the cast of characters to her friends. "Susannah Tierney," repeated one slowly.

"I know I've heard of her," said the other.

"When you come right down to it, why have we been interested in any of Susannah's guys?" Cole continued. "If you forget the razzle-dazzle, they've been a pretty tedious bunch. She's a shameless headline-grabber, don't you see?"

"Oh." I frowned down the row of empty black-lacquer tables and sighed. "Of course. I don't know how we missed it."

"She's always been good at getting talked about," Dee conceded.

"Don't we have anything better to do?" I said. "It's almost enough to shut a person up."

"Well, there *are* other people in the world," said Cole.

So we wondered out loud whether Joey was really sleeping with his friend Fern.

ANOTHER PARTY

$\mathcal{D}$ee Kilmartin, who used to give a lot of parties, was lonely this past winter. Lonely for the first time since boarding school, said Liz Quirk, who always sounds as if she knows what she's talking about. Of course, everyone is lonely and unhappy as a teenager. Look at "young adult" novels: kids locked up, jeered at, tormented, abused, and abandoned. No doubt such books are a great comfort to suffering youth. Unfortunately, there is no ready-made literary equivalent for those around thirty who have lost their friends by moving uptown, which is what happened to Dee. An editorial job at a fine-arts press up on Riverside Drive, a deal on a co-op nearby: it must have looked good at first. She couldn't know then that she might as well have moved to an air-force base overseas; the place was that isolated.

It used to be a standard joke that you couldn't walk a

block with Dee Kilmartin before someone would come up and say hello to her. Up there, even though her new job was partly social (fund-raising; she grew up with money), she never ran into anyone. Liz said that when she was with Dee a couple of weeks after her move, a man with a mustache approached them outside a fruit-and-vegetable market. Dee's arms were full of packages; she put on her smile, and Liz thought, This is the same old Dee after all. But the fellow must have mistaken her for someone else, because he excused himself, and she was left smiling at his back.

Liz told me all this at a Valentine's Day party given in a railroad apartment on St. Marks Place. I was lonely myself, because my friend Cole had been sent to his paper's Paris office to cover fashion, so I asked, "Why doesn't she give one of her parties, then? I miss them."

Liz looked around, obviously about to say that we were *at* a party. But, really, it hardly deserved the name —someone in front of us was pricing earrings in a magazine—so instead she said, "Dee claims it would be no use; no one will come that far uptown."

"It is awfully far away," I said with regret. Dee Kilmartin's parties had been special. Afterward someone would always say, "No one went home alone," which, although not literally true, best summed up the splendid complications that resulted.

After the party on St. Marks Place, all Liz said was "Did you notice that even our hostess disappeared for most of the evening?" We'd escaped to the bar of the

Chinese restaurant around the corner, where, a drink later, a guy told me my eyes were "Veronese green." This piqued my curiosity more than the guy himself did, so the next day I called Dee, who knew all about dead painters. I hadn't talked to her in months, but she sounded her usual unruffled self when she told me that the emerald green named after Veronese had never in fact been used by him. "Emerald green?" I said. "Not exactly the color of my eyes," and she said, "No," and I said, "Everybody, absolutely everybody, is a charlatan." One remark led to another, and we agreed to meet at the Met to check out the Veroneses. Since I was between jobs (I design book jackets, mainly), I had a lot of extra time, and it wasn't until I hung up that I realized Dee would be leaving work early to join me.

I got a little nervous when I first caught sight of her in that big entrance hall. I was light-headed, anyway, from being on the Upper East Side, where everything is so clean and tall that your forehead somehow rises to join in. Also, she looked odd—still quite solid but sort of shucked—because I had hardly ever seen her alone. She tended to move in crowds, bridging gaps in conversations or jumping into them aslant. It was almost a relief for me when, within minutes of our greeting, some kind of spasm passed over her face, she murmured, "Oh, my God," and swung her head around and down, saying, "It's the Mask Woman."

"The Mask Woman?" I whispered.

"Did she see me?" Dee asked her hands.

"I don't even know who you mean," I said.

Then I saw at the entrance a woman in a stylishly oversize red shirt and a long peach skirt slit halfway up the back. She was just turning around to talk to a young man behind her. I could see him full-face, and he looked sick: white face, bluish lips, purplish cast to his eyelids. But for me the woman's clothes were more disturbing. Because red and peach look so strange together, I would never wear the combination in public, but I do have a red bathrobe and a peach slip, so those are the colors I see most often when I am essentially undressed.

"Don't just stand there," said Dee, and I followed her around a corner, into a passageway of statues and sarcophagi. We stood in front of some stone heads on pedestals as Dee explained, "I had dinner with her once. Fredericka knew someone I worked with before I quit my job here, and she was supposed to talk to me about— well, I forget what. Instead, all she did all night was attack me for hiding my feelings. What was I supposed to do then? Cry?"

"Fredericka is her name?"

Dee nodded. "Fredericka Ackerly. But to me she will always be the Mask Woman. Every time I saw her after that, she said I was wearing a mask." This was not such a terrifically bad description of Dee Kilmartin's face right then; her smile was still the one she put on and took off all the time for strangers, as if it were a hat that fit too tight.

"Who was that with her?"

Dee shrugged.

"She certainly likes them young," I said.

"Here she comes," cried Dee in despair.

Sure enough, the Mask Woman was striding toward us, holding out one hand, trailing the boy a half step behind her.

"How pleasant to run into you," said Dee through set teeth.

"It's so hard to tell if you mean that," said Fredericka in a deep, thrilling voice.

Dee introduced me by my first name—Rosemary—but got no further before Fredericka gestured at the kid, gold bracelets clanking. "This is my son, Frederick. He has such a feel for artistic honesty that I hate to go anywhere like this without him."

Frederick—now quite obviously just a teenage boy—looked at us with hate, jammed his hands in his pockets, and walked across the room to another, larger head on a pedestal.

"Frederick finds the social amenities exhausting," said his mother, smiling.

"I didn't know you had a son," said Dee.

"Yes you did."

Even the courteous Dee Kilmartin did not know quite how to respond to that. "I did?"

"I'm sure you knew. It's fascinating what people block from their minds," the Mask Woman said. She had a way of rocking her head back and forth, as if agreeing with herself.

I slipped away with downcast eyes, but Dee didn't follow. With her frozen expression, squarish skirt, and long, dotted scarf, she looked like some exotic butterfly pinned to a board.

Eventually I reached the boy, Frederick, who was still standing in front of the same head. He didn't turn even when I joined him, although I moved in quite close. From there I could tell that he wasn't looking at the head itself but at the pedestal, or maybe the floor. After a few moments I said, "Do you like this one?"

"They practiced human sacrifice," he said.

I said, "The Romans? That's not really true, is it?"

Frederick turned on his heels and disappeared toward the entrance hall.

"Oh, Frederick, honey," called Fredericka from the center of the room. She waved a business card over her head as if to flag him down, then handed it to Dee. "Remember," she said. "This is only for the *real you* to use. I don't want to talk to any old mask." Then she walked quickly after her son.

"Frederick and Fredericka?" I said to Dee when they were out of sight.

"It makes him sound like her toy, doesn't it?" said Dee. "But she's not much older than we are. Mid-thirties at the absolute most."

"What does she do?"

"I think she's divorced."

"Let's at least see a Veronese," I said, and we climbed the two flights of wide stone stairs in silence.

Dee found Veronese's *Mars and Venus United by Love* right off. "He was probably about forty-eight years old when he painted it," she said, and we exchanged a look. To the right of the Veronese was a Tintoretto. "Twenty-two," said Dee. We sighed and exchanged another look.

I was at the next painting first. "This is better," I said. "Sixty-seven."

And so we went down the wall: "Fifty-two." "Between twenty-one and twenty-three." "Twenty-two again." This last was a Titian, and Dee said with great satisfaction, "It's not even a real Titian yet. There's no glow."

We went around the corner and through the other rooms in a flurry of figuring. In front of a Watteau (between thirty-four and thirty-six), Dee said, "You don't think she's right, do you?"

"Who's right?"

"Fredericka. About me. About the mask."

"You can't be serious," I said.

"I've got the perfect cure for all ills," Dee announced when she called a week later. "We're going to sit in the Matisse room at the Museum of Modern Art. It's the most cheerful room in the city." But we'd barely gotten to the second floor before we were at it again: thirty-three; forty-five; seventy-two. This time, though, there were more people around to overhear us, and we didn't find the whole process quite so entertaining. By the time we stopped in the bright, airy snack bar, we'd gotten downright subdued, and the oddness of being alone with Dee returned. It was as if she were a stranger, when in fact I'd known her for nearly a decade.

"So when are you going to have another party?" I asked quickly, as soon as we sat down. The floor was a speckled black-and-white, like the cover of a composition book.

Dee of course said she lived too far away.

I said, "A. Douglas Jackson drives ten hours every weekend to and from someplace upstate."

"So I heard," said Dee. "I also heard he just changed his name to Doug Buckland."

"You're kidding. Where did he get that?"

Dee made a face. "Imagine a party full of Doug Bucklands."

She sat up straight even when she was sipping coffee. Down her back ran a French braid; long, stiff, nubbed, it looked like an extra spine and made her posture seem more correct than it was. Her face is broad, flat, high-cheeked; it is midwestern, stubborn, very pioneer-looking. She is not the sort of person you want to argue with.

"Besides which," she added, "we're too old. There's no one left to meet."

Because of this and like exchanges, I did not at first consider our outing a great success, but evidently Dee did, because suddenly she and I were seeing each other for drinks quite a lot, considering how far away she lived. Liz Quirk had—as usual—exaggerated the situa-

tion a little. Dee could hardly have lost *all* her friends in
the move uptown; I'd occasionally hear what a guy said
to her at the theater or some other place frequented by
couples. Also, Liz Quirk quite out of the blue mentioned
the age calculations to me, so Dee must have described
them to her. Still, you could tell that Dee was basically
lonely—partly because she had a new way of talking
about what was said to her a few days earlier and where
she went last weekend, as if it all had taken place a long
time ago. And partly because—well, who wasn't?

I don't know what had happened to everybody. Cole,
of course, was in Paris. And Liz was usually waiting in a
public place for a friend she referred to as the Soap Star
—obscurely, since he wasn't even an actor; he worked at
a magazine. But no number of individual fates could account for the crowds of people that seemed to have disappeared. The only solution was a party; I just had to
make Dee see that. So, at a lunch place in a cellar near
Times Square—it had a great jukebox and it was halfway
between us—I said to her, "Remember the time we
ended up hitching a ride with a garbage truck as the sun
came up? You and Curtis were both hanging on to the
driver's door flirting with the guy inside."

"I really don't flirt, you know," said Dee. She was cut-
ting a wedge of strawberry pie into tiny pieces.

"Look, I was there."

Dee glanced up, pleased. "Maybe I was flirting just a
little," she said. "He was awfully cute."

"And remember when Eileen was making out with

some fellow on the edge of the tub and they discovered her date passed out behind the shower curtain?"

"You were there, too?" Dee asked.

"Well, I heard the screams."

But Dee Kilmartin wasn't having any of it. "I remember. You were still talking to Curtis, right? But then he left the party with that guy you were after." She waved her plastic knife. "Who was he, anyway? Didn't he live in Eileen's building?"

"Oh, Dee," I said. "How should I know?" But she got what she wanted: I shut up. I watched her finish her pie.

There's a special sort of pang you get when you realize that you aren't going to learn seven languages, and that there are countries you won't ever visit, and that somehow through the years you've turned into a specific sort of person. Liz Quirk told me once that she'd dreamed she died in her apartment. She said, "The problem is, I have such a good deal on this place that the dream isn't just anxiety, it's prophecy." I at least had had sublets for seven years, but perhaps that was even worse: I would eat off strange plates forever.

"Think of all the things that could happen at a party," I said on the phone to Dee around the time of the Derby (colts and fillies—all, of course, aged three).

"I can't think about that right now," she said. "I'm going to be away next week."

"Where?"

"Nowhere real. It's for business. But Fred's going to be staying in my apartment."

"Fred?" I asked.

"You know, Fredericka's son. Apparently someone told her I was going away, and she and the kid need a vacation from each other."

"Oh, you mean the Mask Woman. You call him Fred?"

"He prefers it to Frederick. Many Fredericks do."

I admit I didn't think a whole lot about this call. I had made a new friend named Judy Schooler, who instantly took up lots of my time. Although Dee and I didn't always talk about parties, the topics of our conversations did tend to be limited, so I assumed that despite her isolation Dee must still have other, better friends with whom she discussed everything else. Judy gave the opposite impression: no one was closer to her than you. She had a way of compressing her voice—a subtler equivalent of leaning forward and whispering—even if she was telling you nothing more than the best way to lock up your apartment. I give up facts about myself only one at a time, but I don't think Judy even noticed how reticent I was, so I made a friend in spite of myself. And soon it became clear that in the meantime Dee Kilmartin had made a new friend, too.

It couldn't have been more than a month after her trip that she invited me up to a reception for an illuminated-manuscript something or other. I dropped by the restaurant with calculated enthusiasm (could this be a run-through for a party?), and there he was: Frederick Ackerly, dancing up to Dee, exclaiming, "They've got color Xeroxing next door!"

How old was this kid? But at least his disposition had improved. He showed Dee some sheets of paper, and the two of them smiled at each other as she leafed through them. With Dee, he somehow passed for a normal human being, despite the purple hoods on his eyes. And he had a nice, three-noted, oboelike laugh. Before I left, Dee told me she'd hired him as a messenger; he would be working for the press a few hours a week through July and August. I wondered what it would be like to know someone so young. I thought of the advice I could pass on (Make ice cubes from hot water, and they won't get cloudy.)

I spoke to Dee only once more before the end of the summer. Maybe that was because of Judy. Or Fred (seventeen, as it turned out). But it's also true that the one time Dee and I did speak she said, "You are getting a little hard to talk to," just because I'd asked her if she thought the hostess of a party could marry people, the way the captain of a ship could. Then she went on: "When I was a teenager I started hoping there was some happy alternative to families, and I'm just now remembering why. Fred says his father knows him better than Fred knows himself. It seems that Dr. Ackerly psychoanalyzed the kid. Of course, that was Fredericka's idea."

"Fred's father psychoanalyzed him?"

"Yes, isn't it creepy?" said Dee. "But imagine thinking

that someone could know you better than you know yourself."

When we finally did talk next, in late August, I was the one who called. I was reading a mystery on my sublet couch, when it occurred to me that I hadn't spoken to anyone in three days. This made me nervous, so I started dialing numbers, and the first nonmachine I got was Dee. A phone conversation, if at all intimate, is insistently intimate, since there's nothing but the two voices. Because of this, Dee's tone when she told me she was taking Fred shopping—she was confidential, shy—did not at first strike me as odd. When I hung up, however, I thought: Shopping? Why, I've *lived* with more guys than I've taken shopping. What was going on here?

It was chilling, if you let yourself think about it. I mean, *Dee Kilmartin* and a seventeen-year-old? But I got used to the whole idea fast when Dee called the next day and said, "I want Fred to meet some new people. He spends too much time with his mother."

And I said, "Yeah? What are you going to do?"

And Dee replied, "I'm going to throw a party."

The day before Dee Kilmartin's party was warm, the sky baby blue. Dee was sitting out on her tar-papered terrace with a cup of coffee and an English muffin. As she bent over the fronds of a potted plant to check it for bugs, she felt a shadow move above her, in front of the sun. She looked up; a man was falling between the buildings. Then he was gone. Because another terrace jutted out below her like a huge step, she could see nothing beyond it but more black-streaked brick walls. She called the police, then sat out on the terrace awhile longer with the French doors open in case the phone rang, but she heard nothing more.

Dee told this story at her party, which started out a terrific hit. "I wish I knew whether he jumped or fell," she said. "Do you think I should call the cops to find out?"

The place was packed, so if there were people who hadn't come because they wouldn't make the trip uptown, it was just as well. I'd brought Judy Schooler, who was horrified by the story. "She doesn't even care," she said when Dee left us.

"Of course she does," I said. I was getting a little tired of Judy Schooler.

The terrace was in the back. The front of the apartment was laid out around a large airshaft, and two narrow rooms thrust forward on either side of it like the legs of a Sphinx. One of these was the entryway, where an oval ormolu mirror hung, so that you greeted yourself first thing when you came in and you were the last to see yourself off. Beyond the entryway was the living room, which was large, with a huge teal-blue couch smack in the middle. The other leg of the Sphinx was the kitchen, and at the back of the living room, next to the terrace, were two tiny bedrooms. In one, a young guy with a headful of blond curls slept for most of the night. In the second I found Liz Quirk and Joey and a friend of Eileen's called Tom Barbee and his girlfriend and a whole bunch of others I knew at least by sight. This was a good sign, since it's more fun at parties to talk to people familiar enough to expect something from; people you don't know can't surprise you.

Because you could always pick out the bright-red roses on Dee Kilmartin's high-waisted, full-skirted dress, she seemed to pop up everywhere. Early on, I saw her bend over a chair that held the boy Fred and kind of tweak his nose. They looked so comfortable together—maybe this wasn't such a bad thing, after all—that I thought I'd go over and say hello to the kid, although I still had many reservations about, well, socializing with someone nearly fifteen years younger. (That was a whole other adolescent right there.) I sidled up to him and asked him how he was doing, and he said, "You're wearing the colors of the Italian flag."

Whimsy would have been bad enough, but he spoke with an extreme and baffling hostility.

I looked down at my striped cotton skirt. Was he Italian himself? I wondered. Did he think I was? "Whose colors are you wearing?" I asked.

He sneered.

So I looked around for someone else to talk to, and there by the bar was Joey, who said, "What's new with you?"

"Oh, nothing's new," I said crossly. "As you very well know." It was awfully close. I put my wrist to my forehead.

"Well, I thought maybe . . ."

"What? What did you think?"

"Nothing, nothing. I wasn't talking about anything."

"It just sounded like maybe you were."

"Nothing in specific, I mean."

"I see," I said, looking around.

From across the room we heard "Finish the *hamster* story."

This is what I'd been pestering Dee for? It was hard to believe. I didn't even see anyone drink a different cocktail from usual. It suddenly seemed as if every combination of guest had already been tried, and things had locked into the kind of standstill that meant from now on everyone would be all alone.

But I couldn't go home. Because I'd expected to stay on and on quite happily, I'd let an illustrator I barely knew persuade me to let her use my place that evening. All she'd said about her plans was that the guy she was meeting there was not her boyfriend. The very lack of detail that had interested me so much at first now made me cranky. To try to make my predicament more interesting, I told everyone what it was, but even that didn't help.

There weren't many people left when the crash came, but the noise was so loud, so final, that most of us pressed into the living room, big-eyed. It was the mirror in the entryway. Nothing else would have shattered quite so spectacularly. Although a few shards still glittered like sequins against the grayish backing, there was little of the glass left in the frame. Without a reflection, the room had been cut in half, and the wall looked sadly two-dimensional. "It was that kid," Judy said to me with excitement. "What's-his-name—Fred. He just ran right up and smashed it with his fist. Don't you see what this means? By breaking the mirror, he was breaking himself. You can read a lot of self-hatred into this, if you look deep enough."

"You don't have to look too terribly deep in this case," I said.

A couple of guests were foolishly picking up glass with their hands, and Dee Kilmartin was nowhere to be seen. Judy said she'd gone after Fred.

Then Judy herself left, for a club on Laight Street. "You were right—this was a great party," she said to me before joining some new friends, who were waiting for her in the hall. Soon others started wandering off. I considered going myself, but I wanted to wait until I was sure my apartment was empty.

By the time Dee returned, the party had dwindled to a few small, drunk, and oblivious huddles in dark corners. "Rather an exciting night, wasn't it?" she said, flicking on light switches. Guests looked up, blinking, dazed.

"So what happened to the kid?" asked one with a lightning bolt for a dress strap.

"Who knows?" said Dee. "It's not like there was a trail of blood to follow." But privately, a moment later, she said to me, "The party upset him. He's used to having me all to himself."

"What did you do?" I asked.

She sighed. "I called his mother from a street corner and left a message on the machine. I don't think I had much choice."

Fifteen minutes later the phone rang. A guy in the kitchen tried to answer it, but Dee took the receiver from him as he picked it up. "Hello?" she said. Then: "He's there?"

The telephone is not supposed to ring at a party: everyone who could call should be there. If a call does come in, a small group of guests all listen in, contradict ("I never said that!"), and relay messages ("Tell her I never said that!"). This may be why I was leaning in the arched doorway beside Dee, listening to unselfconsciously to her conversation with the Mask Woman.

Dee was saying, "I wanted to make sure he was all right." She twisted the flesh-colored cord around her forearm as she listened.

She said, "It was a pretty large mirror, actually."

She said, "I don't . . ."

Then she blanched. When she hung up, her face was a blank, as if her features had been erased. Then she was a whirlwind of sharp, snapping noises: the ice breaking out of the metal tray, the ice cracking against itself in the glass, the ice popping apart when seltzer was poured over it. She took a long drink, then set the glass down with another sharp rap. "What is *wrong* with that woman?" she said finally.

"What on earth did she say?" I took an expectant step, and we were alone in the blue-papered kitchen.

"She thinks I'm upset because I wanted Fred to spend the night," said Dee. "You know, not just spend the night but . . ." She glanced at me. "Oh, it's unbelievable."

So I'd been totally wrong about what was going on between Dee and Fred.

"I suppose she was trying to be interesting," said Dee. "I suppose that's why she said it."

At least I'd had the sense not to hint at anything to Dee herself. But I should have known better. People don't change that much, or so I have found, over the years (thirty-one).

"I was just trying to make things a little easier for him," she continued. "He's a good kid. I guess you haven't had a chance to see that."

"I'm sure he is," I said. This lie made us both feel better. As Dee relaxed a little, her features returned.

"Why the Mask Woman gets to have a kid, I'll never know," she said. "It's as if you have to be completely horrifying before you can become a parent."

"Look, even I can tell you how to get a kid," I said.

She said, "No, no. Please. There are so many ways to do things wrong and so few ways to do things right."

SAVING FERN

You have to understand about Liz. She is a lot like me. If you took a bunch of New Yorkers and put them in a room, and first you took away the guys, and then you took away the people born in foreign countries and the people who spent their early years in boarding schools or slums and the people who didn't grow up Catholic and the people who didn't know normal things, like the shape of Florida, and then maybe you took away other people who weren't like us for other reasons, you would eventually end up with me and my friend Liz Quirk. Of course, there are categories that would divide us, too, but that is too lonely a prospect to consider.

So up at the Tierneys', when Liz began to interfere, when it looked as if she'd finally gone too far, it was unsettling. It was as if I'd been reading along in a mystery and I'd started to suspect that the heroine and apparent target, the character I most identified with, was in fact the murderer.

It all started when Liz decided to go up to Ridgefield to visit Joey's old girlfriend Fern. Fern had been living with the Tierneys for maybe four months by then, and to me this made a certain amount of sense. She had given up her rent-stabilized apartment back when she moved in with Joey, so when he kicked her out, she had no place to go. She certainly couldn't afford another place; she was still trying to live off royalties from a book she'd written about her father, who'd known a number of jazz musicians. Susannah and Harry Tierney, on the other hand, had a lot of room in their new house, and Susannah needed the company. Harry still commuted to Wall Street every day, but when they'd left the city, Susannah quit her job to do free-lance design out of the house, and at least once a week she'd be so starved for distraction she'd open her address book to the A's and start dialing. Somehow she got Fern during one of these sessions, and the next thing anyone knew, Fern was up in Connecticut, too.

Liz keeps certain friends just so that she can tell funny stories about them later, and since Fern is, well, amazingly naïve in some ways, I'd always thought she fit into this category. There was nothing amused, however, about the way Liz spoke when she called me.

"They introduced her as their teenage daughter!" she cried. I didn't even recognize the voice at first.

"What?" I said into the phone.

"Susannah and Harry—" she began again, and by this time I knew who it was. "They introduced Fern as their teenage daughter. I heard it with my own two ears."

"Oh, well," I said. "They were kidding."

"The neighbor didn't think so."

Fern is not the sort of person I know anything about. Her mother died shortly after she was born, and her father ran with a fast crowd. She grew up in the Bronx surrounded by grown-ups, one of whom brought her a cow skull from Taos for her twelfth birthday. When she lived with Joey, she kept it on top of the refrigerator.

So I said only, "It sounds as if they were being harder on the neighbor than on Fern. You can always tell when someone's putting you on."

"Rosemary," said Liz. "You didn't see this. It was unbelievable. She's thirty years old, nearly as old as you or I, and she's living like a child." The phone dropped with a clatter. When Liz got back on, she was whispering. "I'm in the study," she said.

"You're still at the Tierneys'?" I asked, but Liz was already hanging up.

Across the aisle from us on the train three men and a woman played bridge on a hard-sided briefcase. "Pass." "Pass." "Pass." "Do I have a choice?" As they threw down their hands, one of the men scratched out a couple of lines with a tiny gold pencil, and they all laughed at something I hadn't heard. Commuting seemed such an easy and happy life, so secure and simple.

"I don't know how they stand it," said Liz, indicating the bridge players with a lift of her dimpled chin.

"Oh, Liz," I said. Liz has a persuasive manner, no doubt reinforced by a job at a magazine in which she tells people what to do all day. Also, of course, she was right. Even if the compartment were always cooled to this exact temperature, and even if the sky were always this clear, chalky blue, and even if you never heard anything less contented than this folding and straightening of newspapers, it would be so tedious to ride to and fro, to and fro every day.

We were on our way to the Tierneys'. I don't know how Liz arranged it all, but it was barely two days after her call that Susannah asked me to come to dinner the next Friday night. Then, within the hour, Liz herself called—from her apartment this time—to make sure I'd accepted the invitation. "I'm going, too," she said.

"Again?" I said. "It's funny, I didn't know you were so close to Fern."

"Oh, there's this incredible sweetness to her," Liz said vaguely. Then she changed the subject.

It wasn't until our trip was nearly over that she said, "You notice I'm wearing my missionary costume."

"Oh?" I said. Actually, she was wearing a black linen dress I'd seen a million times before.

"It took quite a while to assemble," said Liz. "Note the severe neck"—here she began to point to the relevant parts of her outfit—"the long sleeves, the tight belt, the dowdy skirt length—"

"That is hardly dowdy," I said.

"The drab color"—I, too, was wearing black, but I let this pass—"the unfashionable shoes, the *Girl Scout pin.*" This last she bent over to show me, holding out her collar with her thumb. "These are not frivolous clothes," she said. "These are the clothes I'm going to save Fern in."

"Oh, Liz," I said.

"It's got to be done," said Liz. "Or she'll end up with an emotional age of eight. The only question is, How am I going to get her away from there? How can I get her to leave the nest?"

"You could always send her to college, I said.

When we got off at our station, blinking in the bright sunlight, there were two rows of cars jockeying slowly around the far end of the platform. Windows everywhere sprouted arms and heads; horns honked; there were a couple of shouts. Gradually commuters and cars paired off, disappearing amid an efficient slamming of doors. In the end a lone white car came up, but it wasn't driven by anyone we knew, and a fellow who had been sitting unseen on a wooden bench behind us hopped in, throwing a light-colored raincoat into the backseat as he did.

We sat down on the bench, and Liz said, "Look. Susannah is very proud of the house, and she'll want to take you on a tour. All I want you to do is keep asking questions and stuff, so I have a lot of time with Fern."

Instead of answering, I looked around. The station house was boarded up, and there was no phone in sight.

"Well?" said Liz. "Will you do it?"

Liz has always watched over her independence with great zeal; she won't spend two holidays in a row with her parents, and she rarely has two dinners in a row with the same guy. Perhaps this is extreme, but it's all too easy for a woman to slip the other way. "All right," I said. "I'll do it."

After another five minutes, Fern drove up, waving her arm as if there were some way we could miss her. On her wrist was a watch with a face as big as an Eskimo Pie. Her dress, too, was large. When she reached across the seat to open the door, one pretty shoulder was bared by the wide, sliding neck. "How *are* you?" "How are *you?*" "I'm *so* sorry I'm late."

I sat between Fern and Liz, my knees propped up, and thought about how familiar it all was—except that the last time I'd been fetched from such a station, I was fifteen years younger, and my friend picked me up in a car that belonged to his parents, who also owned the house I was going to visit.

Fern even looked like a teenager. She had fine red hair gathered low on her neck and clear young skin and big serious eyes and a part as straight as string. She was slight, too, and just a little splayfooted—a coltish touch. She wore new white sneakers and new white ankle socks, and she drove with her chin up, as if she were having trouble seeing over the dash.

"It's funny," she said. "When Joey left me, I thought I

could never be happy again, and now here I am, as happy as a clam."

"It's the weather," said Liz.

"Yes, isn't it nice?" I said.

"One day the world is caving in on you," said Fern. "And the next day you see there's this door, and you can just step outside and look in at all the mess."

"Of course, there's a difference between getting perspective and running away," said Liz.

"I suppose," said Fern. She did not sound interested. "Did you hear about this guy who chopped his girlfriend's hands off and put them in the freezer?"

"No," I said. I hadn't heard. When was that?

This must have made Fern a little nervous, because she took her foot off the gas pedal and looked at me. "I read it in the newspaper," she said. "I think it's true."

Liz was frowning.

"I like your sneakers," I said to Fern.

"Susannah gave them to me," said Fern. "I wish I could get something for her, but I can never think of anything."

We had turned right at a large white church, and we were now on Main Street, passing a display of gardening tools in front of a hardware store. "Get her a trowel," said Liz. And she continued, as we drove slowly, slowly past the low brick buildings with the burnt-wood signs: "Get her a dress." "Get her a ring." "Get her another dress." "Get her a suit." "Get her a sandwich." "Get her a frame." "Get her a pet."

"She already has me," said Fern complacently, and then we were there.

Even from the road, you could tell that the house was huge. I could hardly believe that people my age owned it. It was white. It was two and a half stories high. It had three dormer windows and a small semicircular portico dripping with vines. It wasn't as old as it pretended to be, but it looked extremely homey, considering its size. And in the front, in the middle of the lawn, stood Susannah, motionless, one hand on her hip. Two sprinklers fanned themselves nearby.

We all piled out, and Fern said, "I headed the wrong way on the street in front of the bank."

I must have expected Susannah to be more matronly somehow, to complement Fern's new role, because I was surprised when she suddenly came to life, grabbed me by the shoulder in her old way, and cried, "Look at me in this place. It's like the crazy people have taken over the asylum, isn't it?" Up close, you could see that her knee-length pants had a leopard-skin pattern. I had forgotten how loud she was.

In the sudden cool of the flagstone entryway, she added, "Not that anyone is crazier than Fern."

The phone rang off to our right, and Fern ran to answer it. "Susannah!" she yelled.

When Susannah left, Liz said, "Well?" and I said that for Susannah "crazy" was obviously a compliment.

"Besides," I said, "I've seen no sign that Fern wants to

be saved. It can't be that bad. Susannah did give her those sneakers."

"That's nothing," said Liz. "Fern has a whole closetful of clothes Susannah bought for her. She's dressing her like a doll, don't you see?"

I said, "I wish someone would dress me like a doll."

Then Fern returned, and Liz said, "So when are you coming back to the city?" and Fern said, "This Tuesday. Susannah and I are driving in to see a play."

Liz said, "That isn't what I mean."

And I said, "Which play?"

But I did what I was told: I asked all sorts of questions as Susannah showed me around the house. This proved more difficult than I'd expected, since the place was so bare. I mean, there were normal things in the kitchen and the living room and the dining room, but in the first room we entered on the top floor there was nothing but a grandfather clock, unwound. I crossed over to it, opened the little door, and asked a couple of questions about how the mechanism worked. "Who knows?" said Susannah.

So we went to the next room, which held only a Chinese brush painting. "That's writing, isn't it?" I asked.

"Something about a nest of vipers," said Susannah. "It was a wedding present."

The next room was even harder, as it was completely empty. The window looked down onto the back patio, where I could see bits of Liz and Fern sticking out from under a fringed umbrella, the kind that shades a table.

"I wonder what they're talking about," said Susannah, suddenly right next to me at the sill.

I guess I jumped a little. "What's in there?" I asked quickly, pointing back across the hall to a closed door on the other side.

"That's Fern's room," said Susannah. "There's no point in going in there. It's always such a mess."

I asked Susannah how long Fern was going to stay with her.

"Oh, Fern is living here for now," said Susannah. "I don't think I could stand this place without her."

Susannah spoke so straightforwardly that I couldn't recall what all the fuss was about. This happens to me sometimes. I will see one point of view and then another almost immediately, as if my mind had the double field so popular in painting nowadays. By the time we got to Susannah's room—or rather, Susannah and Harry's—I felt quite comfortable asking, "You don't think Fern is taking advantage of you?"

"Not at all," she said.

The bedroom was pretty, in a conventional way. All the furniture was white. The wallpaper was Dresden blue with tiny white starbursts. There were pastel dhurries on the floor. In the corner was a rowing machine holding two tidy stacks of magazines.

"I don't mind telling you that it was pretty hard for a person like me to live out here at first," said Susannah. She picked a lint brush off the bed and lay down. "Fern has made all the difference." I leaned awkwardly against the handles of a dresser as Susannah fooled with the brush, balancing it on the back of her hand and trying to flip it into her palm. "You wouldn't believe the ideas she gets. Do you know what she said to me the other day? She said that sex makes you taller. Now, even I realize that's crazy. Although it's true she's the shortest person I know."

"Are you glad you moved?" I asked.

"It's so hard to decide," said Susannah, getting off the bed. "Harry likes it. And you have to grow up sometime, I guess."

I figured that Liz had had plenty of time to use up all her arguments, so I let Susannah take me out to the patio, where Liz and Fern were still sitting. Liz was wearing dark glasses. Fern was holding a straw hat in front of her face. "It's like the lights of the city," she was saying. She must have heard us come up then, because she dropped the hat to her lap and said, "Oh." She ran a hand over her smooth red hair and gestured at a tray of bottles and tumblers. "Liz won't eat citrus fruit," she said.

"I just don't like wedges of things in perfectly good drinks," said Liz, seesawing a little on the edge of her seat.

I'd sat down next to her and stated a preference for lemon over lime before I realized that Fern had been crying. She'd stopped, but her face was blotchy, her eyes were red, and her lashes were stuck together in wet clumps. I could feel the first inkling of tears behind my own eyes. What had Liz said to her?

"I can't believe we need new cushions already," said Susannah. There were pink-and-white-striped cushions tied to the back and seat of each of the iron chairs. Susannah had pulled open one of the split seams to expose the pitted foam rubber underneath. "Incredible," she said. "Rubber rot." When she finally sat down and noticed Fern's face, she said, "What happened to you?"

"Nothing," said Fern.

"She's upset because Debby T. died," said Liz with some disgust.

"Oh, her," said Susannah.

"Who's Debby T.?" I asked.

"You really don't read the papers, do you?" said Fern. "She was a little girl who needed a liver transplant. They used the 'T' to protect her identity, but there were always pictures of her."

Susannah laughed. "Fern is very well informed," she said. "Once she told me interest rates were coming down, and it turned out she read it in her horoscope."

"Oh, well," said Fern. She shrugged. She looked around. She looked at the three-trunked oak tree behind us, at the cluster of rhododendrons by the cellar door, at the long slope of lawn. She said, "I'll be right back." She let herself into the house, fiddling a bit with the French doors first—they had to be lifted, then kicked.

"She really is the funniest person I've ever met," said Susannah. "She can't do anything. She can't drive across town without getting lost. She can't scramble eggs. She can't play cards. She can't choose shoes."

Liz said, "She can speak French."

"She can water-ski, too," said Susannah. "And no one can water-ski. It just goes to show."

I had no idea whether Fern had been hurt by what Susannah had said. I had no idea whether Fern had really been crying over Debby T. It is hard for me to gauge a person like Fern, who is absent in just the ways everyone else I know is insistent.

There was the sudden high whine of a car starting up on the other side of the house. Then there was the squeak of tires as the car pulled away.

"That wasn't Fern, was it?" asked Liz.

"I'd rather not think," said Susannah. "But you heard me mention those cushions."

"Oh, no," said Liz.

I didn't understand this at first, either. I looked at Liz for illumination, but she was once again frowning away in her missionary costume, arms and legs folded. I looked at Susannah. I said, "You mean Fern went to buy new cushions?"

Susannah was embarrassed. "She's always doing stuff like that," she said. "Even when no one wants her to."

Fern got lost again, so it was two hours before she returned with the new cushions. She tied them to the chairs as the rest of us watched. We put off eating until Harry came home, which was late, about ten-thirty.

Susannah kissed him on the lips as he took off his tie. Since the early days of his marriage, Harry had gotten better or worse, depending on your point of view. He was much more sure of himself, so he felt free to make remarks. Some were about Fern's driving, and others were about her clothes. It was disgusting in a way, but it was meant affectionately, and Fern seemed to like it. Her smile kept springing back up like jumped rope.

At one point, when everyone but Fern had finished eating, and she and Susannah were describing their favorite thrift stores to Liz, Harry started telling me a story. First he leaned forward in that proprietary way some men have. Then he said, "We had our bedroom wallpapered a few months ago."

"I saw," I said. "It's very nice."

"That's different wallpaper," he said.

"Oh," I said.

He now had the attention of the others at the table. "Susannah and I had it done just before we left for a long weekend," he said. "And when we got back, it was hanging in strips."

"It wasn't really in strips," said Susannah.

"Yes it was," said Harry. "Apparently the radiator had been disconnected, and the temperature dropped so much the first night we were gone that the heat came on and the paper was steamed right off the walls. What I can't believe is, Fern saw all this and did nothing about it."

Fern laughed. "I walked by and saw all this fog in their

room, so I just closed the door." She made a slamming gesture with her right hand, which was still holding a fork.

"Now, what kind of person would do that?" asked Harry. He was shaking his head.

Fern appeared to be thinking this out for herself. Or at least she wrinkled her forehead and screwed up her mouth. But then the smile sprang back, and she sighed.

"Fern is coming back to the city with us," said Liz.

We all looked at Fern.

"Is this true?" asked Susannah.

"Well, yes," said Fern, bowing her head. "I meant to tell you."

"Incredible," said Harry. He lifted his napkin from his lap and put it on the table in front of him. He crossed his legs, put one arm over the back of Susannah's chair, and tipped back in his own. He had the puffed-up, excited look of someone about to sneeze.

Susannah frowned at him. "Fern is not a normal person," she said. "I don't know how you can expect her to behave like one."

"So she's going back to the city," said Harry, still marveling.

"Of course, I could stay if there was anything I could do to help," said Fern.

"God, no," said Susannah, wilting suddenly. "That's all I need." She picked up some plates and left the room.

I waited for a moment, but Harry didn't have the sense

to follow her, so I was forced to speak in front of him. I said to Liz, "They were perfectly happy, you know."

Liz glowered at me.

Fern said, "I think I'll go pack."

"It's not like this is at all necessary," I said as soon as Fern had left. "You're not responsible for everything in the world."

"Maybe," said Liz. "But if you try to be responsible for nothing, you end up like Fern." She was sitting there very stiff-necked, her little white face as rigid as stone.

Liz and I don't have husbands. We don't have children. We don't have pets or cars or property. People leading a certain sort of expectant life in New York have none of these signs of adulthood, and this is no doubt why Liz found Fern so upsetting. It has always been easy for me to say I'm like Liz. It's harder to admit we both might be like Fern.

So I said, "All right." Then I asked, "What did you say to her?" and when Liz didn't respond, I asked, "How did you get her to see she's got to make her own way?"

"You've got to tell us," said Harry, who was still balancing himself on two legs of his chair. "It's a miracle."

"Actually," said Liz, "I told Fern that she could spend some time with me."

As she spoke, Fern appeared in the doorway. One hand held a wicker suitcase, and the other clutched a straw hat to the back of her head. She had changed her clothes. Her dress was blue, with a flared skirt, puffed sleeves, and a big white collar. It was the sort of dress that a young girl in a thirties movie would have put on for her first trip to the big city, full of dreams of breaking into show business, or helping the poor.

TWO NEW PEOPLE

I didn't realize how many guys worked at Hare's until the day I started work there myself. This was maybe ten years ago, when I first got to the city, and Hare's, as you probably know, is a used bookstore downtown. First off, there was a blond guy wearing a T-shirt the fuzzy, faded color of carbon paper. He opened the door for me that morning using only one arm—his right —because in the other he carried a Styrofoam cup with a triangle punched in the top. And since he was standing to my left, I had to duck under the arch made by his crooked elbow. I felt like I'd been squeezed inside. Then there were a few other guys talking in the front—"Hey, Jim," they said as they saw the guy with the cup—and there was a skinny guy sitting on a step ladder off to the side—he was wearing pointy black shoes—and there was a larger guy taking off his denim jacket at a desk, and there were two guys walking toward us with clipboards, and there was another guy standing in their way. And this isn't even counting all the guys back in the stacks, guys I could hear but not see: "Where's Jim?" "In front." "Where?"

The door banged behind me, and a guy carrying a bicycle pump sauntered in. He nodded. "Hey, Jim," he said.

For a moment, I thought: I have never been with so many guys in my entire life. It was incredibly exciting. At the same time, it was like something out of *The Birds*, when you see birds, birds, everywhere, filling the sky, collecting on wires, lining up on the tops of buildings.

At first it looked like I was the only female in the place, but then I noticed this other person standing over by the cash register with her arms crossed. She wore dark-red lipstick on a large, lemon-shaped mouth and no other makeup. A braid as thin as a shoelace was tucked behind one ear. Her skirt was stylishly black and short, and her sweater was stylishly black and baggy, but up closer you could see she was exposing with some defiance a moth hole in her sleeve the size of an oyster cracker. The guy Jim said, "Oh, *two* new people," and somehow this precipitated an introduction.

"I'm Rosemary," I said, and the "I'm Eileen *Filley*" I got in response sounded like a correction. She stepped forward smartly, extending a hand. Her short high-heeled boots had fringes on them.

Eileen and I turned out to be the only two women out

of maybe fifty employees; we were part of a new hiring policy. This was lucky, as I hadn't considered getting a job anywhere else. Hare's was famous. Boy Bait's keyboard player, Peter Forker, had worked there, as had many other rock-and-roll types who were not quite so well known. I guess I'd never noticed that they were all male.

The owner—a vexed but inattentive type—couldn't decide what to do with Eileen and me. We stood around for close to an hour before he put us downstairs, off by ourselves, in the back. There we shelved books on guns, standing in a short, narrow aisle formed by twelve-foot metal stacks. For a while we worked silently, side by side. Then Eileen said, "I just left graduate school." She pushed up her sleeves and looked at me fiercely. "Without getting a degree."

I was impressed. I said, "Women have to stop going along with things."

"Exactly," said Eileen. "And the more difficult something is, the more important it is that you do it."

We continued this conversation through lunch, which we had at a taco place down on Broadway. The area was incredibly pretty, although I didn't realize it at the time. There were, for instance, several plane trees on the north side of the cross street that were taller than I was, and there was a landmark building on the south side, the home of an old Tammany Hall politician. But I was just out of college, and I was more impressed with the prostitutes who hung out on the street corner. Eileen pointed them out to me as we walked back to the store. Then she told me in confidence that she wrote plays.

After lunch, Jim showed us how to stamp remainders. We were put in the basement again, this time in a kind of clearing by a desk. None of the cartons were stacked more than thigh-high, and you could look across to the stairwell or over to the various concert notices and stuff taped to the wall. We sat on folding chairs. On the desk a fan whirred, stirring up dust. The stampers were larger versions of the kind used in grocery stores—not exactly elegant items—but Jim held his with great gentleness, and in his extra-large hand it looked almost delicate. The technique took only a minute or two to demonstrate, but he hovered over us for a while, sipping from another Styrofoam cup.

Eileen asked, "Are you some kind of manager or something?"

Jim was embarrassed. "Oh, no," he said.

She began to stamp. *Ker-chow, ker-chow.* "Because I thought maybe you were," she said.

"I guess I just like to talk to people," he said. He flashed a quick, sly, diffident, engaging grin. I hadn't noticed before how pleasant he looked, with his broad face and his widely spaced features and his light-colored tortoiseshell glasses. He had the sort of hair that I always thought a man should have when I was growing up: it was thick, and it sprang up and back from a slightly receded hairline.

He looked at us for a while as if trying to make up his

Good Gossip

mind about something. Then he said, "Every day for our afternoon break a bunch of us have martinis across the street. I was wondering if you two would like to come."

"I don't drink," said Eileen. *Ker-chow, ker-chow.*

"Oh," he said. *Ker-chow, ker-chow.* "You're on medication?"

"I just don't drink," she said. She looked up at him and scowled.

Smack in the center of the bar were four tables pushed end to end. This is where Jim sat, with maybe eight other guys from the store. They were the only people in the place, aside from two old men sitting on stools and the bartender, who was filling a couple of juice-size glasses with draft beer. I could see few martinis anywhere, which was a relief. At four in the afternoon, I was better off without one. I raised a hand, palm out, to Jim and went over to the bar.

Along the far wall was a string of bad still lifes—fruit, fish, flowers, wine bottles, one envelope. The colors of the paintings tended toward orange, as if gleaned from television, and the walls were the dark, promising green of an OTB office. The linoleum, too, was greenish, but murky, and worn in odd spots by the pivoting of the lightweight, thick-framed, cafeteria-style furniture. It was a great place, as exciting as Hare's.

The guys at Jim's table were not quiet, and even from the bar I could hear lots of what they were saying. One fellow said about a movie, "Endings haven't been the same since they got rid of capital punishment," and someone else dismissed a new record by saying, "What did it risk? Who did it offend?" It was funny to hear such subjects discussed so harmoniously. The only jarring note came from a fellow to the right of Jim, who wouldn't stop drumming the table with the flats of his hands. He was an odd, narrow person with an overhanging upper lip and, under the ear I could see, several tilde-shaped scars. I couldn't decide whether I liked his looks or not.

As I was sitting down with my beer, Eileen arrived, surprising me as much as Jim, and there were introductions: a Greg, a John, a George, two Marks, all kinds of names. Several people seized the chance to leave, which Jim apologized for, but at least the guy with the scars stopped drumming. He folded his arms across his high narrow chest as if afraid we would try to shake hands. When he was introduced as "Cherna"—his last name, I assumed—he began to tell a story apropos of nothing I could fathom.

"Once I stayed at a hotel built into a cliff," he said. Despite his odd looks, his voice had a pleasant rasp to it, something like the crunch of gravel. "If you opened the top part of the shutters, you could look right down to the sea. Or you could open the top and bottom parts and push them all the way to the side so it was like the room had no fourth wall at all. You could sunbathe on your bed, if you liked. I got a nice tan that way."

Eileen said with some scorn, "You got a *tan* in a hotel

room?" She put her elbows on the table as she spoke, and her sleeves billowed out beside her in big waves of scratchy black wool.

Cherna replied so obliquely that I wondered if he understood the objection. "I am not ashamed to be a poor person," he said. "I was not a tourist, lying around the beach."

"It doesn't matter—" said Eileen.

"Maybe not to you—"

"—you can't get a tan in a hotel room."

There was a pause as they eyed each other.

"Believe what you like—" said Cherna.

"—but drink up," said Jim mildly, looking at his watch. "It's time to go."

We all finished off our beers and rose, pushing our chairs back with our calves. Cherna, who was one of the few who'd had a martini, slid his empty glass down the length of the table with an elaborate hand motion, as if he were tossing a Frisbee. The glass eventually hit an ashtray with a clink. One of the other guys pushed the glass back to the center of the table for no apparent reason—except that he was clearly annoyed. Jim led the way out.

When we were back in the basement of Hare's, stamping—*ker-chow, ker-chow*—Eileen kept looking over at me and frowning. Finally she said, "I always like a good argument, don't you? Is that so crazy?"

* * *

The next morning Jim bought me a cup of coffee. That is, as I was walking in, he was walking out, and he asked if I wanted some. When I nodded, unbuckling my purse, he said, "Forget it, forget it." He returned in a minute or two and gestured me toward the stairs with one of the two cups, saying, "Go ahead. I'll carry this down." It wasn't until he looked into the metal stacks in the front of the basement that I realized he wanted to talk. In handing over my coffee, he somehow made me come to him. Suddenly, we were in conference.

He began by saying, "I've worked here a pretty long time," which was no surprise. You could tell that he was one of the oldest employees in his late twenties, at the very least. Then he added, as if he thought his remark could be misinterpreted as a declaration of some superiority, "Some would say *too* long." It was like Eileen Filley's disavowal of graduate school, except that he wasn't fierce. He was apologetic. "For some reason I often find myself playing peacemaker," he said. "People think of me that way, and it's true—I'm happiest when everyone gets along. Even as a kid, I was always explaining one of my friends to another. If you know people, it's not hard. Insults are mostly inadvertent, I think. Mostly clumsiness."

I sipped some coffee and looked off at the graffiti in the stairwell. His manner was so concerned that he was making me nervous.

He cocked his head; his tone grew mournful. "A person like Cherna didn't grow up with the advantages you or I or Eileen did, and he may be sensitive about unexpected things. I don't think he even wants to be taken literally. It's so unkind to single him out."

"Oh, that," I said. "Eileen didn't make such a big deal of it, did she? I don't remember any fuss."

"I gather she didn't mention it to you."

"She told me she likes to argue."

"Really?" said Jim. "How curious."

The front of the basement was laid out in the same orderly fashion as the first floor. It looked something like a backgammon board, with a wide center aisle and a series of stacks sticking straight out from the walls. It was a good place to talk because you could tell if anyone was close enough to hear you. On the other hand, customers could spot you entirely too easily, and the next thing you'd know, you'd be hunting for books on salt-free diets. This is what happened to Jim, anyway. I still didn't know where anything was, so I joined Eileen in the back, which was full of unexpected turns and corners and extra walls of books.

When I tried to tell her what Jim had said, she reacted with scorn. "Jim is a born collaborationist," she said. "I'm not saying he isn't perfectly sweet, but he'd suck up to a fire hydrant—he can't help it. Besides, insults tend to be insults, in my opinion. Not everything can be explained away."

"Men hate to rock the boat," I said.

"And why did he speak to you instead of me?" she said.

"People are always talking to me. I can barely get a word in edgewise."

But Eileen's scorn got mixed with worry, and she didn't let the subject go all day: "I certainly didn't mean to hurt anyone's feelings," she said as we shelved fiction beginning with *S*. Later, as we moved to *T*, she said, "Office politics at Hare's—who'd have predicted?" and "I always thought men liked women who disagreed with them." After this last, she suddenly stuck her head around a shelf, looked up and down the crooked aisle, and said, "You don't think they're listening, do you?"

Right before four I asked, "Are you going across the street?" and she said, "Yes," as we walked over together, in silence. I noticed for the first time the bell in the door to the bar, which rang as we walked inside. Eileen crossed to Jim's table and said, "How come you guys always get here first?"

Jim glanced at the clock, which was covered with a wire cage like a catcher's mask. "Don't worry," he said. "You'll get to know what you can and can't do soon enough."

By the time I returned with a beer, Cherna had started talking about a trip he'd made to Italy, where the owner of a vineyard asked him for advice on which wine to ship to the States. "Now, I may know something about the subject, but I'm no expert," said Cherna modestly. "What happened was, the guy decided I was the typical American. Me! The typical American!" He shook his head. "And what's even funnier is that he made a million dollars off the deal and invested it in Los Angeles real estate. Which is a far more American thing to do than I could ever manage."

"What wine is this?" asked Eileen.

Cherna shrugged. "The man was obsessed with the United States," he said. "He'd underlined every fact about it in his almanac."

To be honest, I had not thought one way or the other about whether Cherna had ever sunbathed in a hotel room, but Jim's remarks made me consider this vineyard story a little more closely. It probably wasn't true, either, I decided. I couldn't see the point of making it up, but I know that the most sordid invention can be less humiliating than the sunniest truth.

"You are such an incredible liar," said Eileen.

"Wow," said Cherna. He wrinkled his forehead. He squinted. "What makes you say that?" he asked.

"She says she likes to argue," said Jim.

So Eileen looked at me like *I* was the goat, but I didn't get a chance to respond because a guy called George Ess, whom I'd never heard speak, suddenly jumped in and said with some revulsion, "It's better than *wine*-tasting."

You could tell that Cherna was not the most popular of the Hare employees.

Still, he was the one who got the girl. As soon as he and Eileen arrived together the next morning, everyone knew what had happened. Seeing them enter the store was like walking down a city street and catching a sudden, surprising whiff of chlorine or lilacs—it was a reminder of delight. Eileen was smiling; Cherna was smiling. They floated silently down the center aisle. At the head of the stairs, he pinched her cheek, and she cried, "To-om!"

Eileen and I sorted paperbacks according to size that day, which was extremely tedious, but at least I got to hear about Cherna. She talked a fair amount about him, and I liked that in her: she didn't "tell all," but she wasn't coy, either. She took it for granted that I knew.

Apparently Cherna had come up to her on the subway platform after work. There he told her about the secret compartment he'd discovered in an old desk (there was hundred-year-old dust inside), the number of poems he'd memorized (thousands, if you count Christmas carols), and—her favorite—the Silhouette romance he'd inspired. Eileen related all this with great glee, a change in attitude I could not account for until I said, "Well, he certainly has quite an imagination," and she replied, "He told me he's lived in a fantasy world all his life. Isn't it great? He wrote his first novel when he was eleven. It was seventy-five pages long, and it was about men from Mars."

Of course it didn't take Eileen more than the rest of the day to realize that the Martian novel was fantasy, too. But by then she'd got this romantic notion of Cherna's stories: she thought art just oozed out of him. Also, his refusal to separate fact from fiction struck her as subversive, and subversiveness was her goal. Whenever she mentioned a friend with a halfway decent job, she'd have to mention someone else who'd just gotten out of jail or who was living in a box. Being contrary was a matter of principle for her.

Sometime during those first few days we had to carry a couple of open cartons of books to the back of the basement, and when we were finished, we flopped down on them, me rubbing my forearms and Eileen looking gloomily at her legs, which she stuck straight out in front of her. (As the only women, we were not supposed to be carrying that kind of weight, but after the one time we insisted we could do it, no one seemed to notice.)

"Look at those legs," said Eileen. They were extended in front of her, toes pointed, and the black fringes on her boots fell back toward the floor.

"What's wrong with your legs?" I asked.

"Nothing," she said mournfully. "They're so sturdy, so dependable, just like the rest of me."

My laugh was somewhat uncertain; Eileen had a way of saying the funniest things with perfect seriousness.

"You don't understand," she said, and there was a real note of shame in her voice. "I wasn't at all like the other people here when I was a child. I was such an awful goody-goody. If I read with a flashlight under the covers, I thought I was so daring, I got shivers up my spine."

"Kids tend to do what they're told," I said.

"How can you say that?" said Eileen. "Kids are the worst." She sighed. "If I'd misbehaved a little back then, maybe I wouldn't have to work so hard at it now."

She came over to the bar every afternoon that week, but she looked sort of odd sitting there. Maybe it was because she never got herself a Coke or a cup of coffee or anything, and she refused whatever was offered to her. Often she would sit on her hands, which made the place in front of her look even emptier. But you could tell she was having a good time. She would repeat key phrases from everything Cherna said—crying, "A dog that can go shopping for you!" or whatever—and then add, "Where did you get that?" or "You are too incredible."

And Cherna was awfully proud of her. Whenever I got over to the bar before Eileen did, he would be talking about how her voice was so clear it was used in recordings for the blind or how she'd invented Pop-Tarts. All lies, of course, but you could tell he was only trying to convey to us all how great she was. As soon as I'd sit down, he'd say, "Where is she?" and give me this big weird grin.

The other guys who hung out at Jim's table were pretty nice to us, too—nicer than they were to Cherna, really. Eileen and I liked rock music, you see, and most of the guys played in bands or were forming bands or at least had a lot of opinions about bands. It made talking easy. George Ess, who was in two bands at once, occasionally put out a fanzine all in capital letters, and several issues were taped to the concrete wall in the Hare's basement. They were all about how important noise was to a sense of menace, and they inspired a number of agree-able conversations.

Jim was the guy I talked to the most. He was always worried about something; or at least he was always draw-ing me aside. I must say I found this flattering. He was a big fellow, and he had just enough of a slouch to give you the feeling he was leaning into you as he talked. What with his troubled gaze and all that pensive coffee sipping—well, there's nothing more attractive than a person who's paying attention.

His favorite worry was Eileen. His remarks about her were so frequent, in fact, that on my second Thursday at Hare's, when he was waiting for me after lunch, I was surprised that he didn't start talking about her right off. First he looked both ways in the stacks, and then he drew from his breast pocket a piece of newspaper that had been folded up so small it was popping open of its own accord. He unfolded it and unfolded it, and when he finally showed it to me, there were so many creases in it I couldn't tell what it was. "It was up on the wall when I got back," said Jim. "But I think I got it down before anyone else saw it."

By then I'd made out a four-by-five-inch map of the United States on which someone had scrawled a new legend: • ← PLACE WHERE CHERNA HAS BEEN. The map had been almost completely inked in with dots. "Is that so bad?" I asked.

Jim gave me a keen look. "Eileen did it, didn't she?" he said.

"Of course not," I said. "That's not her style at all. She's very direct."

"That's one way of putting it, I guess," said Jim. He took the thing back from me, examined it anew, and said, "Well, I suppose it was done in a spirit of fun. The guys do tease Cherna a little."

I noticed that he had been a lot more disturbed when he thought Eileen was responsible.

Jim put the paper back in his pocket, took a sip of coffee, and pondered something. Then he said, "You have to understand. Cherna comes from the Midwest."

"Oh?" I said. "They tell more lies there?"

Jim gave me a pained look. "I'm from the Midwest," he said. "And I think Cherna is like me. I think he tries to look on the positive side of things. Eileen, on the other hand, is looking for trouble."

I didn't pass this on to Eileen, of course, but she probably would have been flattered. Despite her attempts to be bad, she was still incredibly conscientious. The only person who got to work earlier in the morning was the owner, who opened the place up. I never saw her smile at him; she would have considered that fawning, but she kept coming early, even though twice during that first week she had to wait in front of the store while he went back for his keys. (It was no surprise to anyone when, several years later, he sold the place and moved to Michigan.) She'd lean up against the bony iron grille that protected the front window and shiver, her hands stuffed in the pockets of the crumpled, fringed, black suede jacket she'd bought at a secondhand store to go with her boots. On Friday morning, as she waited, a passing car slowed nearly to a stop in front of her. When she realized that the driver thought she was a prostitute, she ran over and spit in his face.

I heard this story from Eileen before lunch, from Jim after lunch (*"What did I tell you?"* he said), and then again from Eileen during our four o'clock break at the bar, when she filled in the rest of the table. This last time she added, "When I first realized what was going on, the shock of it sort of lifted me up. I saw everything so clearly: I could act or not act. Then I pushed myself just a bit farther—screwed myself up one more notch—and when I ran over, I could have been flying. I never felt so free."

Cherna said, "Once when I was hang gliding this guy made me so mad . . ."

He trailed off as Eileen stood up. She pulled the black sleeves of her sweater over her hands, picked up her fringed jacket, threw it over her shoulder. "I have to go," she said. On her way out, she slammed the door with a great ringing and tinkling of bells.

"What's wrong with her?" said Cherna.

I looked at the clock.

"It's probably time the rest of us headed back," said Jim.

As we were all pushing back our chairs, Cherna said, "Perfume companies pay her to try out their products, you know. It's because she has such perfectly neutral skin."

When I came in on Monday morning, a lot of the guys were standing in front by the cash register, talking about a concert at a place right around the corner—a place full of scarred marble, ripped red plush, and mysterious iron protuberances. The concert had been on Saturday night, and I had been there, too; I'd even run into George Ess in the lobby, and I was surprised at how much pleasure this had given me. It made me feel like I really lived in the city. So on Monday, when I heard him praising the band's use of disruption, I went over and joined in. That is, I agreed. Jim agreed. Everybody agreed. Then somebody told a funny story about finding blood in the sink.

It was all pretty chummy, and I guess Cherna, who was also standing around with us, felt left out. He said, "Eileen and I would have gone, but she had to be in Hartford this weekend. Someone was naming a building after her father, and she was expected to attend the ceremony."

Cherna didn't realize that as we'd been talking Eileen had come upstairs with a sheaf of paper—order forms, it looked like—and she'd stopped over by the center aisle to compare one piece of paper to another, head bent and pencil poised. She must have been listening to us with half an ear, though, because when Cherna spoke, she straightened with a start. "Hartford!" she cried. "I've never been to Hartford in my life!"

Cherna picked up a hardback from the $1.98 table as
if in response. He tried to balance it on his two index
fingers, but it immediately started to slip, his fingers had
to hop madly, and the book slid to the table, pages ruf-
fled and cover askew.

Eileen watched all this with something like horror.
"Listen, buddy," she said. "You may have a life that needs
dressing up for dinner, but I don't. My life is perfectly
fine the way it is, thank you." She stomped across the
aisle and down the stairs to the basement, her angry eyes
shifting here and there, the fringes on her boots swaying.

The guys were pretty embarrassed. You know how
that is: hands that had once been unnoticeable had to be
tucked into pockets, arms were all elbows, and the smallest noise on the other side of the store claimed everybody's attention.

It was the door closing behind the first customer of
the day. Jim, too, was looking in that direction when he
said in a cold, controlled voice I'd never heard before,
"At least she didn't spit in anybody's face."

I didn't exactly know what to say to Eileen when I got
downstairs. I could see her point. But I also wished she
were a little less prickly; it would have been easier for
everybody. So instead of saying anything I simply went
and stood next to her and tried to help her shelve mys-
teries. She was using absurd force—wrenching, flinging,
pounding. She raised a lot of dust. Eventually she said,
"Can you believe that Cherna?" and I said, "I don't see
how you can be so surprised."

Eileen kicked a carton with a pointed toe, leaving a V-shaped gouge. "Whose side are you on?" she cried.

But when I looked at her in surprise, she started to laugh. She sat down on the box she'd kicked and leaned back against a shelf. "I wonder what building it was," she said. "I wonder if I had a good time."

So we ended up talking, after all. ("A lie like that makes you feel terrible," said Eileen, "like you're not good enough.")

I thought for sure that Jim would grab me for another conference sometime during the day, but he didn't seem to be around. One minute I'd notice him in the front, plucking out a book for a customer, and then the next minute he'd be gone. I started to miss that insinuating concern of his.

No one was around when Eileen and I went out for lunch, either, so at four, when she said, "Well? Aren't you coming to the bar?" I happily said that I was.

As we crossed the street, there was a warm, wet, fragrant wind—the sort that lulls you into thinking New York isn't such a hard place, after all—and there was the usual ringing and chiming as we opened the door. Everything looked the same: the orange still lifes, the green walls, the cafeteria furniture, the tiny beer glasses, the dozen or so guys at Jim's table. Cherna was there. The scars under his ear were standing out like salt lines on a boot, but he didn't look too bad. He was staring down at his martini. Jim, on the other hand, looked straight at us as we entered the bar, and as he did, he lifted an index finger and said, "I'm afraid it's that time again—time to go."

Eileen and I stood there, arms akimbo, while all the guys filed out between us.

EILEEN'S NEW PLAY

"Great shoes."
"Great shirt."
"Great room."
"You have such an eye."
"What an adorable muffin."

I was in an agony of recognition, my head lowered, my hand over my brow, as if these lines had seared the theater with bright, blinding light. They were all from one character. (Was she supposed to be comic relief?) From the next seat this guy named Anthony gave me a nudge. "Rosemary," he said. And when I didn't answer, he said, "Are you all right?" So I had to nod and smile under my hand. We were at the final dress rehearsal of Eileen Filley's new play—her first big production—and I had never even met the fellow before. He was Eileen's boyfriend, and she had asked me to sit with him because she was going to be off fighting with the director all night. I had no intention of enlightening anyone who hadn't known me long enough to recognize key conversational techniques. (I did at one party say, "I've heard yours is the most beautiful country in the world," to an Australian, an Antiguan, two Russians, and a Scot. But I also made many uncharitable remarks that evening.)

"You're always so honest."

"He's the best doctor on the North Side."

"No one can read a map the way you can."

When the lights came up for intermission, various people in the sparse audience stood up and greeted one another. Others looked around and wondered who everyone else was. One fellow turned completely around in his seat, like an informer at a political rally. I was in such a state that I said to Anthony, "That really wasn't me, you know."

When I heard his quietly interested "Oh?" I stabbed the air with my index finger a few times, in a vague attempt to show that I wanted to leave.

He followed me up the aisle. We pushed the fire door open together and found ourselves alone in a narrow, uncarpeted passageway. "Now, which one wasn't you?" he said.

The whole situation was getting worse and worse. Anthony could hardly be expected to understand; it was obvious that *he* wasn't any of the characters. In fact, there was no romantic love at all, which was fortunate for him, considering how bleak the play was.

"You can't mean the little girl, because that's obviously Eileen," he said. "And so's the older woman who's kind of looking on. And the older brother, who starts all the trouble—that's really Eileen, too. I know because it's based on something she told me about. And the psychiatrist—that's Eileen."

He paused, but I saw no point in getting involved in this conversation. He pulled the mimeographed program from his inside jacket pocket and began to look through it, saying, "The mother? No."

I continued to look off into space.

"One of the neighbors, maybe?"

There is not much a reasonably polite person can do about a silence like mine. Fortunately for both of us Eileen opened a door at the far end of the passageway just then. A naked bulb in the room beyond illuminated her hair, which was a shock. She'd told me she'd dyed it the sandy brown it had been originally, but I think she'd gone through so many colors in between that she'd remembered her natural shade wrong.

"Has anybody been through here?" she said.

Anthony and I shook our heads.

"I don't suppose you noticed anything wrong," she said.

"On the contrary," said Anthony.

Eileen frowned and pulled the door shut again.

The next time we saw her we were back in our seats, waiting for the lights to go down. She and a guy with a mustache walked down the far aisle, gesturing at the stage. She looked very self-conscious to me.

I didn't take in much of the second act, because I kept my hand over my eyes the whole time, but I think it had more about the girl growing up. At least, I think it was supposed to be the same girl. Afterward, Anthony and I went across the street to wait for Eileen at a Brazilian restaurant that had had a recent resurgence in popularity. Three-foot wooden silhouettes of parrots the color of taxicabs hung from the ceilings. Wooden traveler's-trees stood shoulder-high from the floor. As I sat down I started to make some remark about what a great place it was, but I caught myself in time. Instead I looked around. On a little raised platform in the center of the dining area was a band with two trombones, two trumpets, and one sax, all gleaming, all with smiling half-circles of shadow in their mouths. When the band started to play, I almost said something complimentary about that, too. I hoped we wouldn't have to wait too long. I couldn't say anything good about the play, and I didn't really want to say anything bad in front of the author's boyfriend.

Anthony was looking at me speculatively, as if wondering where to begin. I knew from Eileen that he was some sort of physicist, but he looked more like a slightly shady arts entrepreneur. His slicked-back black hair ran without layering into the nape of his neck, so that the blunt edge of the hair, which was cut straight across, was unusually thick, as thick as a paintbrush. His features were sharp and foxy. He wore a dark-blue blazer with gold buttons, the sort of absurdly dressy casual outfit that makes a man look like he has gone out of his way to dress down.

I think I was the first of our circle to meet him. Eileen likes to imply that she lives in this other, more exciting world of bass players and criminals. Anthony's job must have been a little respectable for her taste, which is no doubt why he was for such a long time "oh, this guy" and then "this guy I met at a bus stop." Gradually he acquired a name, but even around the time I met him, Eileen would occasionally say that a "friend" of hers had done something or other, and while she was talking, you'd realize she meant Anthony. Liz Quirk, who used so many epithets that she would often forget people's real names, still called him "Eileen's imaginary friend."

Anthony said, "You don't look as happy to be with me as I am to be with you."

Did my remarks generally sound as off as this did? I flicked out the white cloth napkin that had been folded in front of me and then tried to fold it back up. "Not at all, not at all," I said.

"It's because you don't know me," he said. "I'm really awfully good company." Now he was complimenting himself.

I glanced up and saw his V-shaped smile, which was full of white teeth. "You must be proud of Eileen," I said.

"It's about time she got the recognition she deserves," he said. "It's been such a struggle for her. Now maybe she'll have the chance to take a nice deep breath or two.

Did she tell you we're thinking of going to Lake Champlain this summer?"

"No."

"Can you picture Eileen in a canoe? It'll be great. Do you know that she hasn't been anywhere but Bethesda"— her hometown—"for three years?"

At that moment, he started to rise, waving one hand, but he soon took his seat again. "I thought I saw her," he said.

It was a woman with similar pale hair who'd just materialized from behind a traveler's-tree, and her posture had some of Eileen's defiance. When I looked back toward Anthony, our eyes met. He said, "She says nothing but nice things about you. I can see why."

This is when I first imagined going to a hotel room with him. Practically speaking, of course, he could have come to my sublet—I didn't have a roommate or anything—but I didn't want him in a place where I'd cooked eggs, washed the windows, put my feet up after work. I wanted a corridor with red wallpaper. I wanted a door that opened with an inviting click. I wanted a rug with a pile as thick as moss.

The next day, I called up my friend Dee Kilmartin, figuring she was the right person to ask. She is very social, and her soothing combination of interest and reserve never changes, whether she's introducing herself or telling you she dreamed she cut herself to ribbons with a chain saw.

"It's Rosemary," I said. "Do I compliment people all the time?"

There was a brief silence. Finally Dee asked warily, "If you did, would it be good or bad?"

I explained about the character in Eileen's play.

Dee laughed. "I don't think you have enough real things to worry about," she said. "*Every*one compliments people more than Eileen does. But what about the play? Did you get to sit down?"

During the performance of Eileen's last play, the audience had wandered around a warehouse with the characters. Still, I assumed the question was rhetorical. I said, "The actress who played me was a little cartoonish, I thought."

"Oh, wait," said Dee. "What was the mysterious Anthony like?"

The shades would be drawn. We would fall diagonally across a white bedspread.

"He's not a bad guy," I said. "We waited in a restaurant for Eileen for about an hour. I finally just got up and left."

"I can't believe some of the stuff Eileen gets away with," said Dee, and I said, "That's because you have such incredibly good manners." It was out before I could stop myself.

I must say I was surprised when Eileen called only a week later. Her play was still in previews, so I assumed she was busy with that. Also, she called so early she woke me up, which was not at all like her. She asked me to meet her for breakfast at a coffee shop on Broadway that neither of us had been to for years. It was a pretty direct route east from my sublet to the coffee shop, and then the coffee shop ran east off the avenue, so when I saw her in a booth in the back, facing the door, I felt as if she'd pulled me there on a string. I also had a funny first glimpse of her: her coffee cup, which was lifted all the way up to her face, looked like a huge, dark, exclaiming mouth. Well, it was awfully early.

I sat down. What I really wanted to do was say to her, "You don't think I compliment people all the time, do you?" and then when Eileen said, "Of course not," I would say, "You're not just saying that, are you?" and she would say, "Of course not," and this would go on and on, with Eileen contributing ever-more appeasing of-course-nots. By the end, however, she would think I was insane, whether she'd originally thought I complimented people too much or not. I know, because I used to have a friend who took to doing this ("Do you think I'm going to make it?" "But do you *really* think I'm going to make it?"), and 'round about the fifth question, I would remember why I hadn't spoken to this person since Christmas.

I also wanted to ask Eileen if Anthony had said anything about me, but this was out of the question. So I said nothing.

Eileen said, "The butter here is that squirt stuff."

I made an assenting noise.

"Do you remember how we used to come here?" she asked.

I made another, similar noise.

"The other day I thought I'd get a real bank account," she said, "the kind with cash machines and branches all over. So I went and waited for about an hour before this account manager saw me. She asked me all these questions, like how long I'd been at my present job, and what was I supposed to say to that? You shouldn't have to explain about your play to get a stupid bank account, so I didn't. She got meaner and snottier, and finally she asked for my passport. I told her not to be ridiculous. I had identification, after all. But evidently I'd stepped over the line. She asked me where my current back account was and then added, '*If you really have one.*' It ended with my tearing the application into little pieces and leaving them all over her desk. It was horrible."

"I see that success hasn't changed you," I said. But as soon as I'd spoken, I realized that it had: Eileen was restless in a way I'd never seen her. Her eyes skittered around the room as she spoke. And when she was finished, she started marking *pi* out of her knife, fork, and spoon.

This was not the sort of exchange I'd expected at all. Weren't playwrights supposed to be obsessed with audience reaction? Why didn't she ask me what I thought of the line "Great shoes"?

Eileen was scraping something off her knife with her fingernail when the waitress came up. "Would you like another one?" she asked, and Eileen said, "Oh, no. No." She quickly put her hands under the table. Her finickiness always embarrassed her. Then she ordered toast, as if that were still all that she could afford. I ordered a normal breakfast.

"Two different Broadway theater owners have expressed interest," she said when the waitress had gone.

"That's great," I said, and then wondered whether this could be taken as a compliment.

"Yeah," she said, not sounding like it was so great. "My parents are coming for opening night, just to persecute me. Last time my mother visited, she was always trying to talk to me in the subway. At least with my father along, we'll take cabs." She sighed. "And Anthony wants me to go on this awful vacation. As far as I'm concerned, going on a vacation is like walking the dog. It's something you get trapped into doing. Anthony of course thinks it's part of a serious relationship."

"Vacations can be fun," I said.

"Are you *crazy*?" she cried. "It was bad enough trying to get a bank account."

I admit I was somewhat taken aback.

"You get settled like that with a guy, and happy, and you turn into one of those little wooden dolls, one of those awful smiling nodding ones with springs for necks." She began to bounce her head up and down in imitation. "You turn into a pea brain."

"I don't see what vacations have to do with it."

Eileen gave me a look.

"I thought writers were always looking at lakes and things."

"There's no point in discussing it," said Eileen. "You wouldn't understand. You like to live with people."

This last was said so mournfully that my first impulse was to contradict her, although I suppose that what she said was true.

"But I haven't lived with anyone in ages," I said.

"Do you remember Dotty Coombs?" said Eileen. "The person who came to one of Dee Kilmartin's parties an hour early? Remember how shy and strange and fetching she used to be?"

I nodded. "She hardly ever said anything, but she had a kind of pulsing silence."

"She came backstage the other day," said Eileen. "It turns out she's married to someone, I forget who. She has a kid, and she's awfully cheery. At the same time, she's harder. And louder. And blander. It's a scary combination."

Was this what she thought of me? I wasn't exactly cheery. But was I bland?

"I can't get anyone to understand," said Eileen. "I try to talk to Anthony, and he says I'll never find anyone better than he is."

"Is that true?" I asked.

She shrugged. "Does it matter?" she said. "I have only one life. I can't fritter it away on anything so silly."

It's funny how a fantasy can take hold of you. I would sit in thrall in my sublet, aware of every cell in my body, but not one particle of my surroundings. Instead I would

see raised patterns on the wallpaper one day, two cran-
berry-colored menus on a table in front of a mirror the
next. Eileen could be lured out of town with a quick
phone call ("Fly up, and we'll talk about a production in
Munich"), and what man could resist a hotel key deliv-
ered anonymously, in a small box? I even had such a box
in my possession: cardboard, cotton-lined, with a picture
of an evergreen stamped on the lid. A young man long
forgotten had given me a single hoop earring in it.

I couldn't concentrate for long, though, because of the
phone. I have scruples; I knew I wasn't going to go
through with any of this, but there is nothing more insistently, jarringly real than a phone ringing. Worse, it was
usually somebody calling about Eileen and her play.

First my friend Curtis called to ask whether he could
get tickets. "I want to bring Bill somewhere really special
for his birthday," he said.

"How did you hear it was so good?" I asked. I mean,
previews of a play like Eileen's go on forever.

He named someone I hadn't heard of.

"Oh," I said.

That was on Tuesday. The next Monday Dee Kilmartin told me that some other people I didn't know had
asked her at a dinner party on Saturday whether Eileen
was as severe as her work.

"What did you say?" I asked.

"Yes," she said.

On Friday, Liz Quirk called to tell me that she'd seen
Eileen on a late-night TV commercial promoting the

play. Fortunately, this turned out to be Liz's little joke, but it did look like "Eileen Filley" was turning into one of those names you have to be careful about mentioning, for fear of appearing to boast. This has happened to a couple of people I used to hang around with; I once went out with an actor who died so well in his first movie that he has been finished off in bigger and bigger hits ever since, but I never knew him as well as I do Eileen.

Then there was the matter of the opening-night party. Dee Kilmartin was buying a new dress—not such a big deal, since she often bought new dresses, but what was I going to wear? The last time I'd needed a dress, I'd worn a short black nightgown (belted), which would have been entirely too appropriate for this occasion, given my ideas about Anthony. And did I even want to go? I told Dee that if I went, I would introduce myself under my character's name only. Dee said, "I don't care what you come as. Just come."

The night of the party I went so far as to rent one of those creaky old English movies, full of whistles—trains, tea kettles, bobbies. But it didn't have a chance. As the credits rolled by, I was already trying to figure out exactly what made a hotel corridor so exciting.

The party was at a restaurant often used for such events. Dee, who had been to other opening-night parties there, had warned me that it was hideous, but by the time I checked my coat (revealing a skirt, not a nightgown), you couldn't see the place behind all the people. They didn't look too happy. I don't know when parties stopped being social and started being business, but somewhere along the way they acquired a certain teeth-gritting uneasiness. It was hard to know whether you were supposed to have fun. You couldn't go over and practice picking up a guy; he was liable to be somebody very important you'd never heard of who'd assume you were looking for an introduction to the stars.

Fortunately I spotted Anthony right away. He was wearing the same dark-blue blazer—an unexpected treat. His hair, too, was the same. (Where *did* he get that shady look of his?) It took me a while to get over to him, though, because Dee Kilmartin wanted me to meet some people who were supposed to give me a job designing a fabulous book on garnishing with vegetables. Plus, she'd just seen the play for the first time, and I wanted to ask her what she'd thought of my character. But I never did get her alone, and when I saw Anthony start moving away, I broke free to join him.

The first thing he said to me was "Did Eileen used to wander around at night?"

"She has always stayed up till all hours," I said.

"So have I," said Anthony. "That isn't what I mean. She's taken to going for walks after she gets back from the theater. At midnight, sometimes."

I shrugged. "She's got a lot to think about."

"I don't like it," said Anthony. "It isn't safe. It's crazy. And what poor fellow likes to be left alone?"

"Hello, dear." This was Mrs. Filley, who had materialized to my right. "Such a happy occasion," she said.

I'm always amazed at how small and fragile Eileen's parents are. Living in the city you hardly ever get to meet your friends' parents, so they take on the larger-than-life outlines of case histories. "They were so disapproving," Eileen would say in passing, and I would think, *Aha*. Or Eileen would say, "They always loved baseball," and I would again think, *Aha*—although what I'd learned, I'm not sure.

Now they stood beside me, as buffed and embellished as a pair of candlesticks. It's not that they didn't look disapproving. It's that they didn't look big enough to affect a person as difficult as Eileen. Mrs. Filley was wearing a pretty, purplish blue suit. Her earrings, pin, and bracelet all matched. People from out of town are always wearing matching jewelry. I don't know where they find it all. Dr. Filley—who was some sort of neurologist, I think—wore a gray suit and a gold watch, and he stood with his hand wrapped around his wife's upper arm.

"You must know Anthony," I said to them, and Mrs. Filley (I couldn't remember either of their first names) said, "Why, no."

She turned to him. "Are you an actor?"

Anthony said, "Ah, no. No. I'm *Anthony*"—although of course I'd just said this—"I'm, you know, a *physicist*." He was shaking her hand with great vehemence.

Mrs. Filley backed a step into her husband. "How interesting that must be," she said.

"I'm at *Rockefeller University*," he said.

"You must be very smart."

"Well, yes," he said. "I mean—"

"It's always a pleasure to meet another man of science," said Dr. Filley, taking his hand.

Anthony was still in shock when they left. At least, his mouth was slightly open. "They've never heard of me, have they?" he said. The crowd thickened around us, but the Filleys were still in full view. They were congratulating the actress who played me.

I said, "It didn't sound like it, did it?"

"It's not that I mind," he said, taking his eyes off the Filleys to shake the ice in the bottom of his glass. "I don't care what Eileen tells her parents. It's a surprise, that's all."

"I never tell my parents anything," I said.

"Shall we sit down?" he said.

Most of the tables around us already had people at them, but there was still plenty of room at the far end of the restaurant, where a raised floor was isolated by a three-rung steel railing. A few dark wooden steps ran up either side. I followed Anthony up the stairs to the right, and he chose one of the smallest tables, which sat six.

Below us the woman who played the psychiatrist version of Eileen fell into a guy's arms. She was wearing a yellow spandex dress as elastic as skin. "There seems to be such a lot going on," said Anthony. "But don't you think that's often only the way things look?"

"I suppose," I said.

"One life must be a lot like another," he said. "Don't you think?"

I nodded vaguely. "What sort of place do you live in? I mean, I've only seen you in restaurants and places."

"Oh, it's an ordinary sort of place," he said.

"A room or two?"

"You'll have to see for yourself," he said.

It was not exactly the invitation of my dreams, but what ever is?

A young man and woman who looked like twins sat down at the other end of the table then and engaged us in conversation ("Do you know many people here?" "*Really?* You know *Eileen Filley?*") until they felt they could move into the seats beside us. That accomplished, they ⲇⲏⲁⳁ ⲩⲣ ⲁⲛⲇ ϫⳙⲥⲧ ⳑⲟⲟⲕⲉⲇ ⲁⲧ ⲩⲥ ⲁⲛⲇ ⲥⲙⲓⳑⲉⲇ

Since Anthony and I were sitting at the railing, we turned our attention back to the crowd below. Most of the plates had food on them already. You could pick out the same three-sided arrangement again and again: a round of salmon, a scoop of rice salad, a crescent of green beans. Dr. and Mrs. Filley were sitting with Dee Kilmartin, I noticed. There were still a lot of people wandering up and down the aisles and hanging over the diners, making remarks. I don't know how the waiters got through.

"There's Eileen," said Anthony, standing. "I'll be right back."

I'd caught sight of her at nearly the same time. She was just on the other side of her parents, one of a particularly tight knot of people by the wall. The rest of them stayed put, though, as she wandered on, stopping every once in a while to lean on the back of a chair. With each gesture, her lenticulated earrings flashed: starfish, skull, starfish, skull, starfish, skull. She still had that self-conscious look—maybe it was something in the way she held her shoulders.

Meanwhile Anthony was down on the floor, trying to work his way up to the wall where he'd first seen her. It was as if the two of them were hands on a steering wheel —as his path arced up and to the left, her path arced down and to the right. When he got to the wall, she reached an empty spot right below me.

"Where's Anthony?" she asked. "Why isn't he with you?"

I tried to point, but she ignored my waving finger.

"He's pretty great, isn't he?" she said.

I sensed a trap.

"Would you like to have him?" she said.

At first I didn't quite take in what she'd said. Then I was very aware of the young couple beside me, silently listening.

"I wouldn't mind at all," she said. "You're much nicer than I am." Why didn't this sound like a compliment? "You'd make a much better girlfriend."

"Don't be ridiculous," I said. But my face went cold, then hot: the idea had been hers long before it had been mine.

Anthony could see us now. He pantomimed laughter (a big round mouth, hand to stomach), then helplessness (a big shrug). He made swimming motions with his arms, as if to part the crowd.

"Well?" said Eileen. "What's wrong? Is it too sensible a solution?"

"Oh, Eileen," I said, but something had lightened inside me. I rose. I called, "Anthony!"

I could tell he heard me by the way he raised his arm: straight out, fingers loose, as if to calm or touch.

THE SOAP OPERA WEDDING

Some people were suspicious of Cole because he always knew what to do. He knew just when to flatter, when to dismiss, when to tease. These strike me as skills to encourage in a friend, but at least one less fortunate man called him "opportunistic," and another asked me at a party, "Does he ever turn himself off?" The trouble was that Cole was flying all over the States to do interviews back when everyone else we knew was trying to sweet-talk his way into a job typing or waiting tables. And that was only the beginning. His byline became prominent, then ubiquitous. He couldn't keep up with all the money he was making; most of his paychecks accumulated uncashed long past the expiration date. Finally the paper sent him to Paris to do the work of three.

It can be as hard to keep liking someone through years of unceasing success as it is through years of unceasing failure, but a lot of people managed it, and I think every one of them called me the day they heard that Cole had suddenly up and quit his job. I never tired of telling the story of his 5 A.M. call from Paris: his voice had been soft, but had sounded close, as if he had been whispering right into my ear. He had said, simply, "I'm coming back."

Here I would imitate a sleepy, bewildered version of myself that I did not truly believe had ever existed: "Huh? What?"

Then I would lower my voice to imitate his conspiratorial whisper: " 'I can't talk. I'm at the paper, and I've got to get out of here. I've quit.' "

I heard nothing more from him for a couple of weeks, but my friend Liz Quirk, who works at a magazine called *Uproar* and so hears more gossip than I do, told me that he quit right after his boss had died, leaving no one at the office but a few French secretaries.

I said, "This is the same Cole who jumped out of a barber chair with his hair half cut when he realized he was late for an appointment?"

"It's weird, isn't it?" she said. "He's always been so pathologically responsible."

"Maybe he got a better offer," I said.

"Nope," said Liz.

"He's just gone AWOL?"

"He's gone bonkers is what he's gone," she said. She sounded as if she approved.

But when Cole did call again, the conspiratorial tone

was gone, and he didn't sound any different than he had the year before, when he'd lived in New York and we'd talked every day and I for one had assumed he'd be at the paper forever. He sounded a little depressed, his voice was lopped off, somehow, but it often sounded like that. I'd never taken it too seriously. He was the sort of person who claimed that he stayed in all the time if he'd stayed in the night before and claimed that he went out all the time if he'd gone out the night before. He told me he quit his job because he hated it, but since when was that a reason for quitting? He was always hating his job, when he wasn't loving it.

I didn't know what to say. I was lying on a quilt-covered king-size bed in a sublet on Fourteenth Street that I hadn't had for long. Reading beside me was my new love Anthony, which made me self-conscious. Finally I said, "You sounded like the bloodhounds were nipping at your heels when you called from Paris."

"I felt like it," said Cole. Then he said, "I don't suppose Frank and Jocelyn ever got married." (Jocelyn had once been attacked by dogs, and Frank had saved her.)

"No," I said. "But it's not like they had any free time. He was arrested for murder and she committed herself to an insane asylum to find the real culprit and then she was kidnapped by a maniac, so Frank had to rescue her again."

Anthony had looked up from his book. "Who was arrested?" he said.

"Frank," I said. "He's on *Light of Our Lives.*"

"Oh," said Anthony, starting to read again.

"Who was that?" asked Cole, over the phone.

"Anthony," I said.

"Oh," said Cole. There was a click. He said, "That must be another call. Let me get back to you."

When I'd hung up the phone, I said to Anthony, "Would you commit yourself to an insane asylum out of love for me?"

Cole and I probably knew more about each other than either of us knew about anybody else. We had been lovers briefly, years ago, although even at the time this had seemed like just one more way of getting acquainted—a way we could soon discard. Afterward we saw just as much of each other. This was back before VCRs, and we'd often watch *Light of Our Lives* together over the phone. Cole predicted the match between Frank and Jocelyn long before anyone else had a clue. And when Cole himself had settled into a string of men, he was the perfect person to discuss sex with, because he couldn't simply contradict me, the way a woman could. Periodically, we would call each other from strange beds; it reassured us that we were the same people from day to day. But now that he was back, all that was changed.

He didn't call for several days, and I couldn't call him; I didn't know where he was staying. Then, when he did call, he asked how my work was going, only to add, "I have a friend Larry who might start designing book jackets." I suppose I should have been put off by this, but actually I was flattered. It's always nice to think of others' wanting to do what you do, especially when you've begun to fear that it's a trifling of your talents. I suggested we all meet for a drink at the Horse Bar.

"He's from out of town," said Cole.

"So?"

"You know how things in New York look to people like that. When I first moved here, I wouldn't take a bath for six months because I was afraid of the paint that had spilled over one side of the tub."

I said, "I thought you had a theory that showers were healthier," but Cole was already going on: "He'd think I was ashamed of him."

"Who is this person?" I said.

"Ned's brother, actually."

"You mean Ned, your old boss?" I said.

"Yes," he said.

"I thought you didn't like him," I said, and Cole said, "Well, I didn't want him to die." Then he told me how he'd picked up Ned's mother at the airport and how they'd sat together in the hospital and how Ned had eventually died in front of them. "His mother kept looking at me, as if there were still something I could do," said Cole.

"How horrible," I said.

"I was offered his job," said Cole. "But when I was making arrangements to ship the body back to the States, I found I was making reservations for myself, too. I was a little nervous about telling the people in New

York I was quitting, but I shouldn't have been; they didn't believe me, anyway. For days they talked as if I had just come back for the funeral. Everyone congratulated me on my promotion, even at the service, even in front of Larry. It was disgusting."

There was a silence as I thought this over. Then I asked Cole where he was staying.

He said, "Someone from the paper put me onto a sublet. I don't know what happened to the regular tenant, and I don't want to know."

"He's probably making a fortune off you," I said. Odd that these should be words of reassurance. "But there's a phone? A TV? An answering machine?"

"Yes, yes," said Cole. "The place is huge. There's room for everything. Even Larry."

"The brother?"

"He's staying with me for a few days."

"Oh," I said. "Do you have an interesting closeness?"

"Don't be ridiculous," said Cole, and I found I was picturing him for the first time since his return—slender, with wide-set eyes and an earnest little ponytail. I hadn't seen him in three months.

"Do you look the same?" I asked.

"I can't tell," he said. "But now that I've quit, I've got the chance to do something different, something more important. What if I've turned into a terrible person? Inadvertently, of course."

* * *

They were an odd pair. Cole—who did look the same, I suppose—was in a handsome dark wool jacket and neat new T-shirt. Larry was in a thick off-white turtleneck sweater, the collar of which was so big it looked like a neck brace. A greasy fan of blond hair fell over his forehead. Both guys were skinny, but Larry was rawer and redder. He stood up when I came in. He looked strong and ill at ease.

The bar Cole had chosen was in a restaurant on the second floor of a brownstone. The recessed walls were the washed-out blue of bank checks, and the white ceramic-tiled floor was inlaid with a pattern of black dots and dashes—dit, dit, dit, dah, dah, dah.

Cole introduced us and said, "We were just talking about Larry's brother."

"Oh," I said.

"He never finished college," said Larry.

"I'm sorry," I said, and then added, "I mean . . ." It scared me, I think, to be with someone who'd just lost a person so close to him.

"So what does one drink nowadays?" said Cole, and I said, "Vodka, I think."

"I finished college," said Larry, "but a beer is good enough for me."

Cole said he would have one, too. Then he said that I designed book jackets, which presumably Larry knew, and I said, "I understand you're interested in doing it, too."

"I could," said Larry.

In a flash I saw that he had no experience in design and almost no interest. "Well," I said.

"I used to have a job, but my boss listened to Christian religious broadcasts," said Larry. "You know how it is."

I couldn't bring myself to ask what his job had been. Instead I fumed. With Larry there, I wasn't even going to get to talk to Cole, and not being able to talk to him was like not being able to touch an old boyfriend.

The next thing I heard Larry say was "I don't think my brother was ever happy, even though he could think of the best things to own."

Somehow the three of us got pretty drunk. When you're drinking, you can either spin apart, so that one person is talking to the bartender and another is using the pay phone every fifteen minutes and another is trying to pick someone up on the other side of the room. Or you can get bound closer together, which is unfortunately what happened to us. Larry had a very mild manner, but he hated just about everything, and the next day, I couldn't believe some of the stuff I'd listened to. Had Larry really said, "Anyone in a position of power has had people killed"?

Cole had been no help. When he described our friendship to Larry, he kept saying, "We watched the soaps together. Months' worth." Although I also considered this a high point, I did not consider it so in any way that Larry would understand, and I didn't like Cole discussing it. Worse, he insisted on ordering an extra drink, saying, "It's for Ned," and then repeating to Larry several times, as if he couldn't have understood, "It's for your brother." The drink sat on a coaster across from me for the rest of the evening, ice melting and bubbles coming unstuck from the bottom and sides until it looked like an ordinary glass of water.

Fortunately I had a few days of *Light of Our Lives* on tape, so I could watch that the next morning. Soap operas are the only things I can watch on television. I like them because they're still raw, as if the scenes had leapt right from someone's idle fantasy onto the screen. *What if I were performing brain surgery and over the radio I heard that the drunk driver who'd hit my child last month was in fact the patient under my knife?* Oh, the temptation of revenge. Oh, the grief. Oh, the sweet nobility of soul. Cole used to say Jocelyn registered emotion so fast that she was like one big quivering lip. Complaining that a soap opera makes no sense is like complaining that the unconscious makes no sense.

After I'd run through the tapes, I drank a Coke and took a test in a magazine entitled "But Does Your Job Like You?" (It thought I was okay.) By then it was after twelve, and I had to either start work or call Cole and find out if I'd heedlessly promised anything to Larry. I decided working would be easier, so that's what I did, and I did the same the next day, but on the third day I started to get annoyed that I still hadn't heard from either of them. What was Cole doing, anyway, that he couldn't call? So that evening I tried him.

Larry answered, and when I told him how happy I was to have met him, all I got from the other end was silence.

I said, "I don't think I told you how sorry I was to hear about your brother."

This at least elicited a response: "I don't think you did, actually." But he sounded thoughtful, not critical, as if he was honestly trying to remember.

"Well," I said. "Is Cole there?"

"I don't know," he said.

So what was I supposed to do now? I said, "Could you go look?"

There was a clatter as the receiver dropped on a table top. When Cole got on the line, I said, "Are you trying to avoid me or what?"

"I'm pretending I'm not here," he said. "People from the paper keep calling."

"Pestering you with job offers, the scum?"

"Sometimes," said Cole. "Or sometimes they ask me what's wrong. As if I had to be crazy to give up all this nonsense. I can't even tell you what they want me to write about, it's so trivial. Do they think life is nothing but yachts?"

I sighed. "Larry didn't really seem very interested in book jackets," I said.

"Maybe you're right," said Cole. "You know, I went out this morning and bought the vile paper for the first time in over a decade. I went into a coffee shop and sat down and ordered blueberry pancakes and started to go through the want ads. There was a little indentation in one of them, a typo, I guess, which made my eyes light on it first. And the job is perfect—at a food bank that distributes supplies all over the city. I was afraid the people there would be too self-righteous, but the woman who answered had a nice raspy voice; I'd say a pack a day at the very least."

It wasn't until then that I realized he'd been going through the want ads not for Larry, but for himself. "You've never looked for a job in your life," I said. This was true: he'd been offered his first job on the paper after he wrote to the theater reviewer, attacking one of his columns.

"Anyone can look for a job," said Cole. "I just don't know what to wear. Everything I own makes me look like a dead person."

"How about the gray pants you were wearing the other night?" I asked.

"Are you kidding?" he said.

He eventually decided to go out and buy himself a new suit. It didn't help. The people at the food bank were so thrilled with him that they immediately showed him their ad campaign and asked for his advice. "The slides were appalling," Cole said later. "It's no wonder they wanted help. But I'm not about to go into PR. There's nothing more corrupting."

Next he applied for a job as manager of a recycling center. But the men who interviewed him, who'd started out as garbage collectors and worked their way up through the sanitation bureaucracy, couldn't understand why he'd take such a cut in salary. One sympathetic fellow said that psychiatrists could be a big help sometimes, and then asked, "Have you, ah, seen any?"

"They thought I'd had a nervous breakdown," said Cole—a bit wildly.

He had no better luck over the next few weeks. A woman made fun of the publications he'd free-lanced for; a man made fun of his accent (which was nonexistent, but maybe that was the problem); and a priest read him a humorous article he'd written about nuns.

Finally Cole resorted to calling likely places picked out of the phone book. At the Suicide Prevention Center, the man in charge screamed, "You could have at least doctored your résumé. Who would believe that a person like you would want to work at a place like this?" Weeks later, an editor at the paper reminded Cole that the center had been the subject of a number of lawsuits.

I don't know what Cole expected, with Larry answering the phone the way he did. It is not how I would choose to impress prospective employers. "I'll have to check" was what he always said when I asked if Cole was in. It got so I cried, "But it's Rosemary!" every time as a kind of booster. Cole ignored all my delicate suggestions about another arrangement. "It's the least I can do for him," he said.

I told the story of Cole's job search to one or two people, but no one was really amused; no one believed it. It's hard to think of a person except in the way you're used to. Liz and I would make remarks to each other now and then, but Cole is not the sort of person anyone would remember to worry about. He's too good-looking, for one thing. And there was still something so eager, so unflagging, so confident about him that you could see why interviewers felt free to make fun of him. One woman at a party I dragged him to asked him what he was going to be when he grew up.

Still, I guess I shouldn't have been as surprised as I was when Liz Quirk called and asked, "Have you had a sane conversation with Cole lately?" This was several months after his return, on a spring day that made everyone look a little unbalanced. (It was hard to tell whether it was really raining, so people kept opening and closing their umbrellas at random intervals.)

"What do you mean?" I asked cautiously.

"You remember Tim?"

"Of course." As far as I could tell, he and Liz gave orders to the same people at *Uproar*.

"He wrote Cole a really nice letter about free-lancing for us," said Liz, "which I don't think is too ridiculous. Our rates aren't too bad; Cole could make ten times the money I do. Besides, he told Tim he was going to come in. But instead he sent that weird guy who's staying with him—Larry. What was Tim to do? They sat down and had some coffee, and this Larry person told him that Cole had decided to do more serious work. He said that the magazine was a joke, but he'd decided to apply for the job himself. I mean, what were we supposed to make of that? This magazine may not be the best in the world, but I don't think it's laughable. Did you see the last issue?"

"I don't think so."

"Everyone said the article on elephants was quite good."

"Oh, God," I said.

"And then when Tim tries to call Cole afterward, who answers but this Larry person, who says Cole can't come to the phone. Tim happens to be a sucker for this, because he thinks all journalists are crazy, but if Cole gets into the habit of sending substitutes . . . well, I don't think everyone will understand."

Jocelyn is always giving out advice, and even though she has been married five times (twice to the same mobster, and once to his son), she's supposed to be the voice of reason. The most I hoped for was not sounding like a fool when I talked to Cole. I called and got Larry, naturally. He said he'd just gotten back from interviewing the star of the play *My Darling Stranger.* Perhaps it was my surprised silence that prompted him to add, "Cole couldn't bring himself to do it and sent me instead."

I said, "Ah. . . . Is he there?"

"He's at the laundromat," said Larry.

"Cole?" I said. I don't know anyone who goes to the laundromat anymore, except to drop off dirty clothes and pick up clean ones. It wasn't ten minutes before I got up, changed my shoes, bought a bag of macaroons at the bodega at the corner, and hailed a cab.

A block west of where Cole was staying was a storefront with LAUNDROMAT painted on the window in a white semicircle. This looked promising, so I walked inside, and there he was, sitting in a row of molded plastic chairs. He was wearing khakis and a dark-green sweater the color of awnings. In one hand was a paperback with a standard repeated-image cover; the other held an ankle against a thigh. He looked so little like a person in a laundromat that I was tempted to try to touch his arm, the way you are with a hologram.

"Hello, Cole," I said, dropping into the chair beside him.

His response was loud enough that two women folding unidentifiable squares of cloth turned around and smiled. Strewn around the floor, I noticed, were white pellets of laundered paper. Machines everywhere vibrated and hummed. The air was warm and sour and pleasant, smelling faintly of baby.

"I brought you a present," I said, shaking the bag. Behind me something metal went *clack-clack-clack* in a dryer.

Cole gently placed the macaroons on the seat beside him, sighing. He was definitely not delighted enough; I might as well have taken the subway. I frowned. Set high in a corner on a pine plank was a black-and-white TV, turned to a soap opera I didn't recognize.

"Just don't ask me about my job hunt," he said.

"Okay," I said. I always forget that an unhappy friend is not exactly the same person he was the day before, except that he suddenly lacks a good listener or a couple

of hundred dollars. An unhappy friend is a pretty prickly
sort.

"I thought I could at least give away money," said
Cole. "I started a new policy of giving it to anybody who
asked. So yesterday on Sixth Avenue, when a guy asked
me for a quarter, I gave it to him. Then he went over and
showed it to a bunch of college kids standing in front of
a bar, and when they started to laugh, I realized he was
one of them. I went home and got back into bed."

"Did you really send Larry in to talk to Tim?" I said.

"I don't see any difference between me and Larry," said
Cole.

This kind of nutty talk made me nervous. "You don't
honestly believe that," I said.

"I got a few more breaks, that's all." He got up and
started pulling heavy wet white things out of the wash-
ing machine in front of him.

For some reason this made me cross. I said, "What are
you doing here, anyway?"

"My wash," he said.

"I don't see why."

Cole said, "Someone's got to do it." Just then he pulled
out the white turtleneck sweater that Larry had been
wearing in the bar. Neither of us mentioned it.

One Friday about a month later I got a call from Cole,
who said, "You'll be in this afternoon?" and, as soon as I
said yes, hung up. Of course I was going to be in; it
looked like Frank and Jocelyn were finally going to get

married. But let's face it: this marriage would be only one more twitch in an endless restlessness. Besides which, I could tape the show, and I hadn't seen Cole since that day in the laundromat. Anthony took up a lot of time. (On top of the many hours it takes to live your life, you need a few extra to tell someone else all about it.) Also, it's hard to admit that you're worried about a person because he does his own wash.

I was throwing open the windows when the buzzer rang. It was a cool, clear day, as fresh as cut grass, and it is always a thrill to listen to steps on the stairs. The top of Cole's head, when it appeared on the flight below, looked sweet and vulnerable, its straight white part begging to have something dropped on it. He must have felt my eyes on him, because he glanced up and said, "It's time for the soap opera wedding!" Still he was coming closer: he was in his tuxedo; he had two large blue plastic bags in his hands. "I've got the whole kit," he said, coming inside and looking this way and that for a place to rest his purchases.

There were two paper cones of white tulips, two cold wet bottles of champagne, two clear bags of collapsible plastic champagne glasses (one of stems, one of bowls), two rolls of white streamers, one paper wedding bell the size of a top hat, a half dozen cucumber sandwiches wrapped in tin foil, and several books of matches on which Cole had written *Frank and Jocelyn, June 10, 1989*.

I think I started to scream.

"It's all part of the new unselfishness," said Cole.

"Oh," I said. "Does that mean Larry is coming?"

"Larry went back to St. Paul." Cole started to twist the streamers and tape them to the top and bottom of my sublet bookcase, which was full of sublet books on how to make money.

"What's made you so happy, all of a sudden?" I asked.

"What makes you think I'm happy?" he said. "It's funny how mad you can get at someone you're trying to help." He opened the bell and looked around for a place to hang it.

"You could try the switch on the lamp," I said, pointing to a torchiere behind him.

This is why his back was turned to me when he said, "I've gone back to the paper."

"What?" I said.

"They're giving me more freedom," he said. "And not only unpleasant things are true. Don't you have any folding chairs?"

"Of course not," I said. There weren't any chairs at all, except for the stool in front of the drawing table.

"Well, we'll just have to sit on the couch."

"Let me get dressed," I said.

My sublet had the spatial arrangement of a TV-dinner tray: three tiny rooms—kitchen, bathroom, and bedroom—lined up in a row against the living room. I was in the bedroom, putting on my silk dress—the one with the star print I always wear to weddings—when the phone rang. It was Liz Quirk. "So I'm a dummy," she said. "I thought Cole had really quit."

"He did quit," I said.

"But now he's back."

"Now he's back."

"The word going around is that he pulled off quite a coup," said Liz. "They say he played those people like a pinball machine."

"People will say anything," I said. But I looked at the slice of Cole that was visible through the crack in the door and felt a sudden awful doubt. How can you really know anyone?

Then I heard him call, "It's starting!" and everything went back to normal. When I hung up, I put on the pink sandals I always wear to weddings.

In the living room, as I bent my neck forward to fasten the clasp on my grandmother's topaz brooch (for fruitfulness in marriage), I said, "Everyone is admiring your brilliant maneuver with the paper."

"I know," he said. "People keep calling and congratulating me. It's so disgusting."

I nodded. I sat down and accepted a glass of champagne.

It was a pretty nice wedding. When the minister asked if anyone knew why these two people might not join in holy matrimony, one of Jocelyn's ex-husbands stood up, but instead of saying anything—and he could have pointed out that he'd forged the divorce papers—he went outside and had a heart attack alone on the steps of the church.

THESE PARAGONS

"If you quote a person out of context more than three times in a single conversation, then you're in love with him." Anthony said this to me once when he was tinkering with his clock radio. I remember I was watching him with my chin cupped in my palm, but I forgot how the subject came up. I was certainly not quoting anyone to him; Anthony Szabo was the only person I was quoting at the time, and I was doing it constantly. I had fallen hard. "Anthony says you can tell a person's self-esteem by how well his doctor treats him," I would say to a friend. "Anthony says he would never travel to a poor country," I would say a few minutes later. "Anthony says it's going to rain."

It was weeks before I realized that I didn't really agree with a lot of what I was repeating. Considering he was a scientist, Anthony had a fantastic sense of personal responsibility. For instance: "Blaming someone else for anything in your own life is sure to wreck it." I said this to a jeweler friend who was complaining about the subways, and he looked at me like I was crazy. Okay, so maybe the circumstances didn't quite fit—this was a problem I'd run into before in my eagerness to apply a couple of months of Anthony to the whole world—but the look set me thinking: What was wrong with a little blame? It took a lot of pressure off a person.

So I told Anthony how I blamed my parents for my need to please and my inability to imagine a successful pairing and my general malaise, and I told him they blamed me for ruining their college years by being born and their later years by growing up.

"I didn't notice you having any trouble pairing off," said Anthony, which was very gratifying.

We were lying together in his studio apartment, on his folded-out couch, under blue-striped sheets that I'd recognized in a movie recently. The top half of the wall in front us was all windows, a long band of them, about fifteen feet wide and four feet tall. The place was like a glassed-in porch, or observation deck, since it was unusually high for the West Village. Built into the wall just under the windows was a radiator scattered with all the different parts of things that Anthony was going to fix.

"Besides which," said Anthony, "if I blame my parents for what went wrong, do I have to thank them for what went right?"

This observation was hardly relevant, since I couldn't

imagine two more blameless people than his parents, but when I pointed this out, he said, "You haven't even met them yet."

So I said, "Something tells me you don't appreciate your parents as much as I do."

Just listening to Anthony talk about them could bring tears to my eyes. His father was in pediatric administration at a Methodist hospital. (Does anything sound gentler?) His mother was in charge of the local Head Start program. When Anthony broke a windup helicopter by slamming it through the glass top of a coffee table, his parents went out and bought a new helicopter. Later, when he had his first hangover, they bought him a hard-boiled detective novel. In fact, they bought him any paperback he wanted. They used to go away if Anthony or his brother gave a party in the basement. They never lost their tempers. And what made this even more extraordinary was that they had had their own disappointments. They'd always wanted to go to Africa; they'd even thought that his father's snooty Aunt Louisa was planning to give them money to go, but it hadn't worked out as they'd planned.

So forgiving! So understanding! I was always imagining conversations with the Szabos in which various details of my life were exposed, examined, and accepted. Religious people probably imagine similar conversations with Saint Peter. Sometimes I'd be lying next to Anthony as I fashioned a few pithy remarks about, say, why I'd lived in sublets for the last ten years, and I'd think, "Wait a minute. I have the perfect audience right here," and I'd try the remarks out on him. Mainly, though, they'd stay in my head, where Anthony's parents would nod and smile and laugh in all the right places.

My own parents Anthony had already seen in the flesh. They came to town a few weeks after I started going out with him, and the four of us had dinner together. This, I swear, is word-for-word part of our conversation.

MY MOTHER: Rosemary had lice.

(I think my father had just been saying something about getting a dog, but the subject did not seem to come up so much as descend suddenly from above, like a beer bottle dropped from a window.)

ME: I never had lice.

MY MOTHER: Well, you did get rid of them right away.

MY FATHER: Rosemary ought to know whether she had lice or not.

MY MOTHER: But I know she never went back to a certain person's apartment.

ME: What person's apartment? When was this?

MY MOTHER: I think you were there just once. For a drink.

MY FATHER: No one told me anything about this.

MY MOTHER: You don't remember when she went to Dr. Antwater?

ME: *Atwater*, Mother, *Atwater*.

MY MOTHER: It must have been around a holiday, because she was home.

ME: That was scabies, Mother, not lice.

Anthony could not see what was wrong with this exchange. He thought it was funny! Of course, with parents like his, how could he understand what seething, spiteful, nervous, fragile, unhappy types most people's parents were?

"You wouldn't want to trade, would you?" I asked, and Anthony said, "I used to hear that all the time from my friends."

Then he said, out of the blue, as we were lying there, "Let's go see them."

"Your parents?" I said.

"Yes," he said.

"Now?" I said.

"This afternoon," he said.

"Just drop in?" I said.

"We could call first. It won't take more than an hour and a half to get there, and we can spend the night."

I sat up in order to think better. "I can't wear that sweater," I said. "That's the one that makes me look like a windmill. I'll have to go back to my place. Maybe I can stop somewhere to get a decent nightgown. Do you think they'd be frightened by my new earrings?"

I first saw the Szabos in their living room, surrounded by their masks and sculptures and fetishes—beautiful things, most of them, especially one standing figure with a flat cat face. You couldn't help wanting to clasp its night-stick-size trunk in your hand and rub its glossy dark surface with your thumb. Suburban houses tend to have the odd brass gong or rattan elephant; this means that the owners have been on a trip to a foreign country. At Anthony's parents' house, it looked like the trip had taken over.

"Most of it is from Cameroon," said Mrs. Szabo, who had told me to call her Jean.

"From outside Yaoundé," said Mr. Szabo, who had told me to call him John.

"It's so lovely," I said, trying to lean away from Anthony on the couch.

"My parents have always liked Africa," he said.

"Oh, really," I said, as if he had not told me the whole story already.

"For years," he said.

"How interesting," I said.

Mrs. Szabo smiled and inclined her head, as if acknowledging a compliment.

"I hope you're not an idealist," Mr. Szabo said to me. "It's better not to have to go through the cure." My ears perked up at this, but he had spoken in exactly the way I'd have expected him to: there was no trace of bitterness in his voice.

"Oh, John," said Mrs. Szabo, smiling, admonishing. "What will she think of us?"

They were sitting on chairs of different heights and

styles, but their postures were the same: each had one hand in the air and one hand on an Old-Fashioned glass, one foot pointed forward and one pulled back. (Anthony, in contrast, was so close to me on the couch it was like the upholstery was breathing.)

Mr. Szabo said, "I always thought maybe one of my children would go over there, but it didn't turn out that way. Instead they live in the gayest places in the world, Anthony in the Village, and William in the Castro."

Anthony didn't seem to find this peculiar, but Mrs. Szabo said, "They're beautiful neighborhoods, of course," and Mr. Szabo said, "Beautiful, beautiful."

"William is a carpenter," Mrs. Szabo said to me.

"I know," I said.

Mr. Szabo said, "Isn't it strange, to have one brother be a carpenter and one brother be a physics professor? But we're strange people, I guess."

Mrs. Szabo said, "He's building a deck for the mayor's son."

Actually, it was hard to believe that the Szabos could have two sons in their thirties. Mr. Szabo had the happy jowls and evenly flushed cheeks of a baby. Mrs. Szabo had lots of lines around her lips and eyes, but instead of aging her, the lines gave her a twinkling star of a mouth and seemed to lift her eyebrows, making her appear unflaggingly interested, surprised, quizzical. They behaved, really, like teenagers in love: they kept exchanging glances; they had constant, irrepressible smiles. Perhaps this is why, despite their solicitousness, I felt just a little as if Anthony and I weren't expected. Besides, there was freshly folded laundry on the chair in the entryway. It looked great; the towels, for instance, were stacked up (green, green, peach, peach) as if they were part of a store display, and the men's underwear was as white as a flash of teeth in the sun, but it was odd, because nothing else was out of place.

At dinner, which was turmeric rice, chunks of fish, and strips of leek, the Szabos started to praise each other outright. "Your father was so different," Mrs. Szabo said to Anthony, and Mr. Szabo said, "I went out with all sorts of beautiful women—actresses, models—but I got the prize, and it was all because of Africa."

"Oh, John," said Mrs. Szabo, looking down modestly at the peculiar food on her plate. (Was it supposed to be African, too?)

"It's all I ever talked about, and it made me fascinating."

Mrs. Szabo offered me a basket of bread with knots in it. "Speaking of Africa," she said to Anthony. "Your father's Aunt Louisa wants to see you after dinner."

"Why?" said Anthony.

Mrs. Szabo shrugged. "You know she doesn't speak more than two words in a row to me."

"Aunt Louisa is very . . . exclusive," said Anthony—pretending, once again, that I didn't know all about this—and I said, "I have a couple of relatives like that."

Mr. Szabo said, "My Aunt Louisa came for Thanksgiving once and ate nothing but a small dish of olives. It turned out she was going to another Thanksgiving dinner later."

"She didn't want to spoil her appetite!" cried Mrs. Szabo. She was twinkling all over: her mouth was twinkling, her eyes were twinkling.

Anthony said, "Generally, though, she wouldn't come, and when all the relatives got together, there would be two topics of conversation. One was the Kennedy assassination, and the other was Louisa. I think Uncle Ralph really hated her."

"Ralph could never take the long view," said Mr. Szabo.

"Didn't she tell him he was a sneak and a liar?" said Mrs. Szabo.

"Well, he *was*," said Anthony.

The Szabos all roared with laughter.

"I suppose you can tell how obsessed this family was with Africa," Mr. Szabo said to me. "Anthony grew up thinking that Albert Schweitzer was just about the most important person in the world, next to his father, didn't you?"

"It's the truth," said Anthony. He was watching his father the close way you watch a race you've put money on.

"And what did I say when I'd come upon you unexpectedly?"

" 'Dr. Livingstone, I presume.' "

"Which was more familiar—'England' or 'the Congo'?"

"The Congo," said Anthony, still watching.

"I'd dreamed all my life of going there," said Mr. Szabo. "When Anthony started kindergarten, I left my job at the insurance company and started to go to school, too, to get a degree in public health, with a specialty in tropical medicine. It was going to be a squeeze, but Aunt Louisa surprised everyone by saying she would give us a little something."

This sounded a lot like the story that Anthony had told me, but I couldn't believe it was; I couldn't believe his father would actually tell it to me.

Mr. Szabo continued, "She was my mother's little sister and not really all that much older than we were, but already her husband had died and left her with all this money, and no children to spend it on."

"You should have seen her car," said Mrs. Szabo. "It had seats made of Yugoslavian calf leather."

"As far as I was concerned," said Mr. Szabo, "the only question was how big the check would be."

Now, finally, Anthony was giving me a look: it really was the same story, only a longer version.

"I took to driving over to Louisa's in the evening. Not every evening—I wasn't a bother—but every third night or so. We would talk on the porch. She really liked opera, I remember. Once she gave me a revolver that had belonged to her father, and once I fixed a loose connection on her phonograph. Sometimes she would ask questions about Africa, and I was always happy to answer. I lent her a couple of books. I was always reassuring when we discussed the dangers. After several months of this, she said, 'At least you're going to have your grandfather's gun. I'm glad I was able to give you a *little something.'* I wish you could have seen my face then, when I realized we weren't going to get any money from her. That was true comedy."

"We did get to Africa, though," said Mrs. Szabo.

"When the boys finished college!" shouted her husband, as if this were the punch line to a shaggy-dog story.

I know that these are not unusual events. I've heard so much about what didn't happen to the men of my parents' generation that I wonder if any of them got what they wanted. Liz Quirk's father wanted to be a doctor but ended up a chemistry professor. Judy Schooler's father wanted to be a doctor but ended up a dentist. Joey Bertrand's father was diverted from private practice into corporate law. My own father wanted to be an artist and wound up a person in charge of salesmen. Usually, though, these disappointments were deeply buried, and you'd hear about them only from the impatient, blithely indiscreet offspring.

I said, "What did you think of it when you finally got there?" and Mrs. Szabo said, "It was everything we had ever imagined it to be."

Outside, as Anthony started up the car, he said, "They like you."

"I like them," I said. "I knew I would."

When we'd driven up from the city earlier that day, I'd

seen a calm old town stiffened with the cold. There had been hills, hedges, beautiful white houses like the Szabos', fields ringed with bare trees. Now the head-lights picked out other, odder things and isolated them: a mailbox shaped like a goose, a sign saying GOOD-BYE LAKE. I tried to imagine Anthony growing up there, but couldn't, perhaps because when he pointed out various things in the dark, I had to imagine them, too.

After fifteen minutes of this, I said, "I'd expected to meet these paragons."

"My parents?" Anthony cried.

I nodded.

"They just know how to have a good time," he said.

"But why should they be so good-natured about this Aunt Louisa?" I said. "Why don't they insult her right back?"

"I don't think they'd be very good at it," he said. He pointed to an indistinguishable section of the road. "That's where I found the Huffmans' dead cat."

But I pressed on. "Don't they have any feelings?" I said, and Anthony said, "They don't seem to mind things the way some people do, if that's what you mean."

Aunt Louisa lived in one of those small cities just over the county line that had never gotten unfashionable enough to be rediscovered. I doubt that the neighbor-hood, with its sweeping elms and buckling sidewalks, had changed in the last thirty years. Aunt Louisa's was a dark, Queen Anne–style house, set closer to the street than the more modest bungalows on either side. It was taller than it was wide, with a two-story circular bay on the left and, on the right, a wide porch that ran around to the back. The elaborately turned porch posts and balusters were white, as were the brackets and the window trim and the many-toothed friezes. All of this decoration glowed a little, skeletal, in the dark.

"Pretty fancy, isn't it?" said Anthony.

"I like your parents' house better," I said.

Anthony had pulled up to the side, but we walked around to the front, where a pimpled white lamp flickered. There was a lace panel with a cat pattern in the sidelight to the right of the door. Anthony buzzed, and we waited in the cold until we heard a train whistle in the distance. Then Anthony rapped the heavy brass knocker once, twice. He looked at the backs of his hands, and we waited some more.

Finally the door opened, and an old woman stood there, looking off over our shoulders as if somebody more interesting were walking up the drive. She had tight brown curls and a tight little mouth and a blotchy face as tough and round and wrinkled as a walnut. "Anthony," she said in a voice that was still high and clear. "This was your grandmother's. I want you to have it." She handed him a cigar box secured with rubber bands. Then the door started to close, and as it was closing, I cried out. (You understand that even I was surprised at my outburst and at how cranky I sounded.) I cried out—and I should also point out that the door shut in my face on the last word—"Aren't you even going to invite him in?"

Well, Anthony thought this was hilarious. "I thought you hated her," he said as we picked our way back to the car. "And now you want to share a nightcap?" When I gave him a look, he said, "Don't worry. She can't hear me."

The first time Anthony spent the night at my latest sublet, on Gansevoort Street, we had the same dream, about finding our way around a lake. Actually, his dream involved a cliff and a car and some other stuff, and there was more of a mystery in mine. But the overall progression was the same, and that was a good thing, because I took it as a sign that we were fated to be together. Otherwise, at times like these, I might have had grave doubts.

When we got back to his parents' house, the kitchen was all clean—it seemed whiter than before—the dishwasher was humming away, and the Szabos were watching the eleven o'clock news in the little room under the stairs. Mr. Szabo's legs were stretched out on the coffee table in front of him. Mrs. Szabo was wearing a quilted silk bathrobe and rose-colored slippers. The paper in her lap was open to the crossword puzzle. It seemed to me that I had never seen people look so comfortable.

Anthony said, as he sat down beside them, "Aunt Louisa gave me a necklace made of shells, and Rosemary yelled at her."

The Szabos looked at me with great interest. "Really yelled?" said Mr. Szabo.

"Whatever for?" said Mrs. Szabo—eyebrows raised, as usual.

"Tell us everything," said Mr. Szabo. And to Anthony he said, "I am in awe of people who can let themselves go like that."

I don't care how uncomfortable sofa beds are supposed to be; Anthony's was wonderful. Because the windows were so low, it seemed higher than other beds, and when you were on it, facing a thick band of sky, you felt perched in an aerie. Plus there were those rolled blue arms on either side to hold a person in place. Buoyant, safe—this was also what being in love was like. Anthony and I would lie there with all the lights turned off, awake for hours into the night. It never got so dark you couldn't see. Sometimes I would look around at the parts of things on the radiator and at the clothes piled up on the chair and at the two-inch halogen light clipped to a shelf above it, and I would think about Anthony and what his life had been like before I came along and what it was like now when I wasn't around. It was as if I'd been turned into a teenager again, marveling at the existence of different consciousnesses. I'd stopped having imaginary conversations with his parents since that first visit, but that didn't mean I'd stopped thinking about them, too, as I lay there.

I had fun when I was with them. At the same time, they made me uneasy, kind of the way you feel when you're attracted to a married man. We went to the ballet;

we went to the track; we went to a restaurant I'd never
heard of called the Forty Winks. I laughed so hard at one
dinner that I almost choked. Afterward, Anthony would
say, "I think they had a good time." I don't remember
being asked about what sort of time I'd had, but every
once in a while I'd tell him how much I'd enjoyed myself,
because he so obviously liked to hear it and because it
made me feel good, too. Besides, what else could I have
said? The Szabos were open and friendly. (That's bad?)
They didn't hide how much they loved each other.
(That's so unusual?)

Once, after Anthony and his father had been fighting
over who was going to pay the bill for a Mexican dinner
that was pretty cheap anyway, Anthony told me that he
always wanted to make things up to his parents and that
he never could.

"What things?" I said. "Your parents have a great life."

"They do, don't they?" said Anthony, pleased. "They
have a fabulous life."

I was being disingenuous, of course; I'd assumed right
off that he was talking about how they didn't get to
Africa. The subject didn't dominate conversations the
way it had at first, but it was one of the running jokes of
the family. Mr. Szabo would say it was harder than it
looked to sacrifice a well-paying career for an altruistic
one; he'd tried. Or he'd say such a choice was too expensive for an "ordinary man." Of course, neither he nor his
wife thought they were in the least ordinary, and Africa
was a kind of proof.

When I asked Anthony why they didn't go over now and work in a hospital, if they were still so obsessed with the place, he just laughed. I knew that this was a habit he'd picked up from his parents, and it annoyed me a little, but it worked; my question did suddenly seem to me ridiculous.

It may sound like Anthony and I saw his parents all the time. We did. But I didn't notice this at first, because I was doing so many other things I'd never done before, like going to parties given by physicists. By the time I'd been going with Anthony for six months, I'd already been to six social events with physicists—seven, if you count Anthony's lecture (*Chaos, Something, and the Strange Attractors of Turbulent Flow*), during which I thought mainly about how he would look with a mustache. I may not have seen Anthony's parents as often, but if it was five times, that's still a lot. Most people in New York see their parents twice in an entire year—once at Christmas (or whenever they're seeing them because they can't see them at Christmas) and once when someone dies or gets married. My own parents met Anthony because someone whose relationship to me I never did figure out got married at St. Patrick's Cathedral.

Perched in Anthony's dim apartment, wrapped in the blue-striped sheets, and looking straight out the window as if it were the windshield of a car, I said, "Do all physicists see their parents as much as you do?"

He said, "They live so close, and they like to go out so much. What else can I do?"

I could have said it didn't look like he trusted them to be out of his sight for long. Instead, when I turned toward him, I noticed that he had the same high forehead and pointy nose as his father, and for a minute, Anthony seemed to peer from behind these features the way you would from behind a Halloween mask. I don't know how a person can be expected to shake a parent, with those kinds of odds against him.

I first met the Szabos in January. Aunt Louisa died late in May. Apparently she'd known she didn't have long to live and so had distributed a number of treasures among her younger relatives, including a broken telescope (to Anthony's younger brother) and a stuffed shark (to Anthony's cousin in the navy). Anthony had passed the shell necklace on to me, and I wore it to her funeral.

The service was held not far from where Louisa had lived, in an old stone church with a generically Protestant name. There were boxes rather than full-length pews, and instead of kneelers, a few large red cushions on the floor. There were maybe fifteen people scattered about. Anthony and I sat halfway back, with his parents. Anthony and his father were on the inside, Mrs. Szabo was to the left of her husband, and I was to the right of Anthony. Mrs. Szabo leaned over both men to squeeze my hand when we arrived. She whispered to Anthony, "We still think she's such a peach." Then the service began.

Anthony had been unusually quiet on the drive up, but

his parents were exactly the same as always. As we sang "Faith of Our Fathers," Mr. Szabo leaned over Anthony to point to one of the verses, then smiled at me. I couldn't tell what he meant, but I smiled back. Mrs. Szabo saw this and opened up her twinkly smile on both of us. Anthony kept singing, studiously ignoring us.

There was a small gathering at the Szabos' afterward, which surprised me a little, since I was under the impression that Aunt Louisa hadn't been to the house in some time. Spread out on the dining-room table was an odd mix of curried lamb, fried eggplant, lentil soup, and cabbage rolls. "You made it all yourself?" said an elderly woman named Helen Ann Fickett, looking baffled. She bit at a piece of lamb with a lunging curve of teeth.

"I love to cook," said Mrs. Szabo. "And Louisa and I had our differences, God knows, but she was still family."

"She was never one for spices," said Mrs. Fickett, taking another bite of the same piece of lamb.

Mrs. Szabo nodded politely and said, *"John."*

"Jean," said Mr. Szabo, who had just appeared in the doorway, arms outstretched. I've never seen two people enjoy each other more.

"Louisa believed in plain American cooking," Mrs. Fickett said to me.

"They say funerals are for the living," I said.

Mrs. Fickett nodded. "This one certainly is."

Relatives who aren't your own look as random as people at an airport. Helen Ann Fickett, it turned out, was some kind of cousin of Louisa's. Heavy-limbed, tiny-featured, with finicky little smocking at her collar and cuffs, Mrs. Fickett looked nothing like the two skinny, envelope-nosed sisters who glided fishlike behind her or like the boy with the red, red lips who sat by himself in a chair near the food or like the stretch-wrapped type talking to Anthony or like Mr. Szabo, who came up and winked at me.

"I hear she left all her money to that boy in the navy," Mrs. Fickett said to him.

Mr. Szabo nodded.

"It doesn't seem fair," she said, eyeing the inside of a cabbage roll with suspicion.

"We didn't expect anything else," said Mr. Szabo.

"Why's that?" she said.

Mr. Szabo put his arm around my shoulder and said, "You haven't heard how Rosemary yelled at her?"

Oh, I knew what this was. I knew it was a trifle, a fancy, a joke, but it chilled me to the bone. I said, "This is where I bail out." I wandered into the living room, which was still empty, and sat down amid the statues and masks and thought about how a story like that could become true in a family. One thing about forgiving a person, I noticed, was that you got to blame him first.

I could hear Mr. Szabo's voice from the dining room. He was loud and a little self-conscious. He sounded like a guy pretending to be Santa Claus at an office party where everybody knew perfectly well who he was. "We don't care," he was saying. "We think it's great."

A DIAMOND

𝓦hen I spotted Eileen at Dee Kilmartin's birthday party, she was part of a tableau at the far end of the living room. First there was a guy, facing out, hands in pockets; then there was Eileen, also facing out, hands on hips; then there was a rubber plant in a large terra-cotta pot. The guy was six inches taller than Eileen, who was six inches taller than the plant. The arrangement was static in the way a bad painting is static: none of the figures had any relation to the other two; each stood stiffly alone. For the guy, this made sense, at least aesthetically. In his green plaid pants, short-sleeved shirt, and bow tie, he had the dated, unreal look of one of the winners pictured in a sweepstakes circular. I assumed that his attire was ironical, but this sort of dressing down is so difficult to respond to. Self-conscious or not, he looked a little goofy.

Eileen Filley, on the other hand, looked trapped. Oh, she had her fierce black jeans on, and her fierce high-heeled boots and her fierce striped railroad shirt. And it certainly wasn't unusual for her to stand by herself at a party. But she was hanging her head—a sure sign that she'd been getting lots of compliments. My friend Cole said she'd developed the habit because flattery was the one thing she couldn't argue with. All I know is that the several people who came up to her and ricocheted away made her fierceness look like a response to a physical assault.

By the time I joined her—it took a while, because Dee's parties are always full of people you have to decide whether to offend—Dee Kilmartin herself was there, introducing Eileen to the fellow in the bow tie. I did not catch his name. Dee said, "He did the music for *My Darling Stranger*, which is just down the street." She meant just down the street from Eileen's latest play, which had moved to Broadway.

"How do you do?" he said, offering his hand.

Instead of taking it, Eileen grabbed my arm and said, "I'm fine, but Rosemary looks like a ghost. See how white she is." She pulled me across the room, through several conversing couples.

I didn't mind, because being pulled through a party always makes a person feel important, but in the back bedroom, under a plate from Audubon's *Quadrupeds of North America*, I said, "All right, what's going on?"

Eileen stopped sorting through the jackets on the bed. "The usual," she said. "I must have stood by that guy for half an hour, and he wouldn't say one word to me until he found out who I was."

I made no attempt to stifle my laughter. "That's the *point* of an introduction," I said.

Eileen snorted. "I can't bear it another minute," she said. "We have to get out of here."

So we went to Sammy's, which is a bar on Eighth Avenue where theater people hang out. Eileen nodded to several men as we walked to our table, and when we sat down, I made the mistake of saying, "I always forget how many people you know."

"They don't know me at all," she said.

"Oh?" I said.

"All they know is my work," she said. "That's the only reason they like me."

"That's like saying people like you for your money," I said. "But I think you have to be very, very rich nowadays to have someone like you for your money." I thought this parallel was a delicate way to suggest limits to Eileen's celebrity. I mean, we were not exactly surrounded by the screaming multitudes. In fact, there was an actress in the corner who really was famous. (I recognized her from the movies, and I never recognize anyone.) Nobody was tearing the clothes off her back, either, but there was a certain stiffness in the way people at the tables near her sat that showed they were very much aware of who she was. At the tables near us, people were as relaxed as old towels.

"Rosemary," said Eileen. "It's not that simple. They make up some tawdry fabulous person in their minds and like *her*. I always feel like I'm going to disappoint them. Thank God I don't have to worry about that with you."

"Because we've known each other so long?" I said. I was not going to go into the less complimentary possibilities.

"We were both nothing when we met," she said, "and I didn't know what a luxury it was. How can I ever be sure of anyone again? Unless I re-create the past." With one hand, she made a ponytail of her hair and threw it over her shoulder. Her hair these days was long, thick, and multicolored: it changed from brown to blond around her eyebrows, where she'd gotten tired of dyeing it.

"What do you mean?" I said.

"I'm going to start posing as my young self."

I shook my head. "Oh, Eileen," I said. "Thirty-four isn't so old."

"I'm thirty-three," she said. "But that's not the point. What I'm going to do is pretend' to be unsuccessful. I'm going to be in disguise, like in a fairy tale. Like when the princess dresses up as a beggar and goes out among her people to find the one good man—the diamond in the rough."

I made a face.

"Don't you remember how exciting everything used to be?" she said. "How anything could happen?"

Against the wall behind her was a velvet curtain. Once, many years earlier, Eileen and a guy she'd just met made out behind it while I tracked down the waiter for the last call. Eileen was always doing things like that when I first knew her: she was wild because she thought she ought to be, so there was always something sweet and ingenuous about her odd crushes, her rude remarks, her single-mindedness. "We used to think we could get away with anything," I said with real regret.

"I just need a small favor from you."

"No," I said.

Eileen started to eat the ice from her tonic and lime. She said, "Even now every time I see a 'help wanted' sign in a window, my heart leaps, and I have to remind myself that I don't need to worry anymore, that I'm not endlessly looking for a job. But what if next time I go in and apply? I'd need a reference, a well-coached one. How about it?"

The scheme was ridiculous, of course, which is probably why I gave in so fast, and why I dropped by so soon to see Eileen at the greeting-card store where she'd found a job. (No one ever did call me about her.) It was her second day, and she was sitting behind the counter on a stool, legs crossed, multicolored hair hanging down, and an impossible grin on her face.

She was not exactly in disguise. She had an expensive

gold ring made of two panthers eating each other up that I noticed she had not bothered to remove. Nor had she discarded the black flats she'd had made for her in Florence. But she did have that grin, and she'd recovered her stare. I'd forgotten how disconcerting it could be. It was part of the posture of defiance she had so assiduously cultivated over the years, and recently it had been disappearing under an answering barrage of acclaim. Now it was back—bright, steady, unexpected, like two headlights on a beach.

There have been times when I've been so filled with dread—on my way to make a presentation to the vile Mr. V., for instance—that I've been almost faint with envy—envy of the token clerk taking my money, the janitor pushing a broom behind me, the driver of the subway train thundering past us. How carefree their lives look then! When of course such jobs must be pretty awful. What I really want to be at those times is a cashier like Eileen—successful, yet not having to live up to my success. Even seeing her there behind the register, I felt a momentary envy tweak my heart. Every flick of her hair, every turn of her wrist, seemed to say, "I'm getting away with it!" If it had been my store, I'd have been sure she was robbing me blind.

"Can I help you?" she said.

"I hope so," I said, eager for some reason to join in.

"If you're a customer," she said, "you're either a tourist, or you work in one of the new office buildings nearby."

"Then I'm a tourist," I said. "That should be more fun."

"No, you answer phones in an import-export office," she said.

She might as well have made up the store, too, which was still in its original, pre-colorized form, with gray linoleum, lighter gray walls, and darker gray countertop. Times Square was right around the corner, but the place was not at all sleazy. It was dusty instead, and a little worn out. The metal stands for the cards creaked as they rotated. The best-sellers I had never heard of. The little balls of fur with eyes held banners in foreign languages —evidently a fad that had never caught on.

Eileen said, "I have a little old lady boss, who keeps saying, 'I'd rather wear a snowsuit in Hell.' She'd rather wear a snowsuit in Hell than do almost anything."

The front door jingled, and in walked a little (five feet or so) old (sixties, I'd say) lady (she was wearing pearls and a cardigan) boss. She said, "Eileen, let's ring out the cash register together. Just for a thrill."

I started to laugh, I was so pleased at the way Eileen's words had called her in. It looked as if the whole world were falling in with Eileen's plans. So it was no surprise to me when she called one morning less than a week later and cried, "Bingo!"

"You found a diamond?" I said.

"A man and I had a nice chat," said Eileen. "I said he had a hard time parting with money, and he said I had a hard time accepting it."

"That was it?"

"You wouldn't believe how sweet it was, actually. Then

he asked me if I'd be here at six. So I said we'd be at Curtains."

"We?" I said. "Curtains?" I said.

Curtains, it turned out, was five blocks away from Sammy's. Sammy's had an empty aquarium in its window. Curtains had a stuffed lizard. Sammy's was identified in green neon script. Curtains was identified in blue. Sammy's had a boarded-up fanlight above the door; Curtains had a crumbling bas-relief of grapes. Sammy's was laid out in a T shape; Curtains was laid out in an L. Sammy's had a long old bar with a railing for your feet; so did Curtains. Both had red plastic banquettes, shoulder-high wood paneling, and black-and-white tile floors. Both had fast clocks advertising brands of beer. Both had photos of Broadway stars above the pool table. Curtains even had a curtain against one wall.

"But this looks just like Sammy's," I said.

Eileen struck her forehead with the heel of her hand. "Rosemary," she said. "Sometimes I despair of you."

I looked around again.

"It's an outrageous rip-off," said Eileen. This last appeared to be addressed to the waiter, who'd just approached.

"Yes, no point in coming in here," he said.

"Two for drinks," she said. I sort of moved behind her, as she stared openly but without interest at all the customers. "There's no danger of my being recognized *here*," she said.

The diamond in the rough, whose name was Teddy, arrived almost as soon as we sat down, so Eileen once again became embroiled in negotiations with the waiter. We switched tables twice because somebody next to the second one was eating fish. At the third table, she must have been struck with the fear that she was slipping out of character, because she turned to me and said brightly, "I think they'd do this for anybody, don't you, Rosemary?"

My voice was equally bright. "Even for someone as unimportant as you, Eileen," I said.

Fortunately, Teddy didn't pay attention to any of this. He sat where he was put, with his legs wide apart and his arms behind his head. "How do you like working in that store?" he asked.

"It's okay," said Eileen.

I was surprised to see how right they looked together. They were both short and sturdy, and they were handsome in the same geometric way—Eileen with her very round face, bisected by bangs, and Teddy with his long forehead and square jaw. She was wearing black bicycle pants; he was wearing a camouflage T-shirt. For a moment, it was as if the whole romance were there in enchanted 3-D, just as Eileen had envisioned it.

"I was surprised to see a woman like you working there," he said.

"How do you mean?" she asked. She was watching him intently. She was also perched as if ready to flee, both hands on the little black pocketbook in front of her.

"The place is much quieter than you are," he said.

"I suppose so," she said, pleased. She threw her multicolored hair over one shoulder. We all watched the waiter set our drinks on the table. Then Eileen said to me, "Teddy bought a set of recipe cards today."

I don't think I had ever heard Eileen make that sort of conversation-starting remark before.

"How curious," I said.

We both looked at Teddy.

"They're incredibly funny," he said. "They show a woman tipping a ladle of sugar into a bowl. Something about the way the sugar sparkles really cracks me up."

Eileen said, "If you own things just to make fun of them, then you own too many things."

Teddy turned a little red, and I could tell he was attributing the moral superiority of poverty to her.

"Where are you from?" I asked him.

"California," he said. And then, looking pointedly at Eileen, he added, "When I first came East to go to school, I thought that everyone here was poor, because all the houses were made of wood. It made me less shy." His smile here was shy, as if to illustrate his point. I could see why Eileen found his manner so disarming.

"Women never seem to have that problem," he continued. "They're always so self-contained." He turned to me and said, "Don't you think?"

"Oh, I don't know," I said.

"Don't get me wrong," said Teddy. "I think they're more interesting, too."

Eileen said, "But we think you're pretty interesting, and you're a man."

"No, no," said Teddy. "I don't mean that. For conversation, a man and a woman are equal. But a woman's history is always more curious. Every woman leads a double life."

"A double life," I said. "What an intriguing hypothesis."

Eileen tried to quell me with a glance.

"Women are more generous, more empathetic. But this makes them more vulnerable, so they conceal their true self, or ritualize it. What is a beauty salon, after all, but an accepted way for women to take care of women?" Surely I'd heard this somewhere before. Or maybe it was my reaction that was so familiar: I was impatient. I was still confident there would be a good part, and I wanted to get to it.

"I love women," he said. "I can't help it."

"I'm sure they love you, too," said Eileen. The irony in her voice was so gentle, I was amazed.

One summer a long time ago I was a candy striper. It was more liberating than I could ever have imagined. Ordinarily you have to be wary of people for many different reasons, but in the hospital I could be as sweet as pie all day long, and it was clear even to my teenage self that this was not because I was ambitious or fearful (or, for that matter, empathetic in my womanly way). It was as if I'd been given a license to be kind. Eileen, it seemed, had been given one, too.

She said, "I am not at that store because I like to take care of people, you know. I am not without ambition."

"Oh?" said Teddy.

"Surely, you, too . . . ?" she said, and when he didn't pick up on this, she said, "A person can have a vision that is larger than his livelihood. In fact, I'd say the larger the vision, the harder it is for society to accommodate it."

"Of course, of course," he said.

"What do you do, anyway?" I asked.

"Rosemary!" cried Eileen. "What a question." She turned back to Teddy. "Tell us about California," she said.

Teddy opened his hands above his head. "There are great murals on the sides of the buildings in Los Angeles," he said. "There was a whole Chicano art movement—"

"Oh, God," said Eileen, suddenly ducking behind the hand with the panther ring. "It's someone I know." She peeked out, using a fanlike motion of her fingers, but even when she'd covered her eyes again, you could see her large lemon-shaped lips and her multicolored hair. She was hard to miss.

"I thought no one came here," I said, trying to figure out which of the people by the door had just arrived.

"He's with a woman who's not his wife."

"A business acquaintance, no doubt," I said. I still couldn't tell who she was talking about.

Eileen shook her head behind her hand. "They'd be at Sammy's then."

"They probably don't want to see you any more than you want to see them."

"Perhaps not," she said. "But they'll come over here, anyway." She dropped her hand, straightened her shoulders, and picked up her handbag as purposefully as you would a weapon. "I'll be right back," she said.

When she was gone, Teddy said, "What was that all about?"

"She saw someone she knew."

"So I gathered," he said.

The couple Eileen stopped was not so different from any other. The woman was certainly the younger of the two, but she was also the more severe. Her elegant black suit could have stood up by itself, her hair was drawn back so tightly it might have been painted on, and she carried two books under one arm—serious stuff, judging by the austere graphics. The illicitness of an affair looked like an intellectual choice for her, just the sort of choice Eileen would make.

"That's the kind of skirt I used to look up as a kid," said Teddy. His face was in profile; his eyes were focused at a distance; his mouth was contemplative.

"My God," I said. "You're Teddy Warren."

"Why, yes," he said. "I am."

You must know Teddy Warren, the male artist who paints so-called women's subjects, like kitchens, laundry rooms, beauty parlors, even ladies' rest rooms. (There's always been a lot of speculation on whether these last were done from life. He would never say.) The appeal is a bit that of the transvestite revue: the surfaces are scrupulously rendered; the finish is glossy.

"I just read about you in one of those art magazines," I said. He was divorced, if I remembered correctly. "This is an honor," I said.

"I hope your friend thinks so," he said. "She has a lot of opinions, doesn't she?"

"A surplus," I said, as Eileen strode up, sputtering, "I hate it. I just hate it."

"Eileen . . ." I said.

"I hate it when very successful men go out with women who are still trying to make it." She threw herself into the banquette beside me, catching me smartly on the thigh with her purse. "She took every dumb thing he said completely seriously. I think she was memorizing it all."

Teddy's face was guarded. "You can't always tell what's going on from the outside," he said.

"Why do people always try to explain away a man's glaring ego?" said Eileen.

"Why do people always assume that the baser motive is the more important one?" he replied.

"Eileen," I said. "This is Teddy Warren."

"Yes?" she said. The name obviously meant nothing to her.

"This is your happy ending," I said. I tried to explain who he was. When this got nothing but a frown, I turned to Teddy and said, "This is *Eileen Filley*."

"Rosemary . . ." said Eileen.

"The playwright?" said Teddy Warren.

"*Yes*," I said.

"Wow," he said with awe. "When I mentioned a double life, I meant it metaphorically."

Eileen was scowling. I never read any of the tales she based her adventure on, but something tells me that when the prince and princess were made known to each other, neither glared the way Eileen did. Nor did either start patting himself down the way Teddy did, feeling for things in his pockets and running his hands over his bare arms, as if to make sure he was still there. You could tell that both he and Eileen were thinking back through their conversation to see if they'd said anything too stupid or revealing.

"I don't get it," said Teddy finally. "Why do you work in that store?"

"Well," said Eileen. She caught me looking at her with anticipation. "I like it," she said.

Teddy nodded to himself. "A woman has to be nice sometimes," he said. "And your plays are full of vitriol."

"Oh, don't be ridiculous," said Eileen.

"But it's wonderful," he said.

Eileen finished off her tonic. "Rosemary looks like a ghost," she said. "I've got to get her home."

"There's nothing wrong with *me*," I said.

I don't know whether Teddy Warren really didn't notice this exchange, or whether he just pretended not to. He said, "I've been planning to work in a soup kitchen

Tuesday nights. I got all the information and everything."

Eileen sighed. Then she said, "It's not that I don't think that's great."

Despite their new wariness and embarrassment, he couldn't disassociate her from virtue, and she couldn't shake her kindness. They eyed each other again.

"I know a couple of people who volunteer there already," said Teddy. "But they're women."

It was weird. I felt like I couldn't lift my glass of vodka, or recross my legs, or even move my head much, for fear of tipping some balance I couldn't quite gauge. I cleared my throat in that sort of strangling way you do when you're trying to be quiet.

"I'm going to have to quit that job," said Eileen. She looked out the window, at a boy on a bike. Then she stood up, pulling a pair of green sunglasses from her purse. "I'll see you around," she said.

Teddy nodded. "I hope so," he said.

He and I were left looking at each other across the table.

By the time I was out the door, too, Eileen was already at the crosswalk, waiting for the light to change. There is something so vulnerable about a person who doesn't know he's being watched; you can't be sure what will happen. It touched me, to see Eileen like that. And when I drew closer, she still looked uncertain, unsettled. She looked as if her clothes itched.

I touched her on the shoulder and said, "What's the story?"

She turned her dark glasses on me, saying nothing, so I tried again. "He's just like you," I said.

But she was already turning away. "Well, that's not very interesting, is it?" she said.

A SUBLET

The place was too good to be true. It was on the second floor of a brownstone—the front half—just off Central Park West. You walked into an embrace of wood at the doorway, and then there were wooden baseboards and a wooden arch into the tiny kitchen and floor-length wooden moldings around the bay windows and wooden shelves built into the wall and a wooden mantel and fireplace. The wood was dark, but reddish, like cherry or mahogany, and it gave the small living room a surprising heft. The bedroom, which was narrower and more delicate, had a long shuttered window and two twin beds with matching dust ruffles. This is where a girl named Debby Bresselman and her mother had slept until Debby went off to college.

Debby Bresselman was twenty-six years old and already married and living on the other side of town when her mother died, leaving her to deal with the lease. Debby didn't know anything about her legal claim to the apartment, she said to me a couple of months later, as we sat opposite each other on the creaky little wing chairs, drinking wine that she'd taken from the refrigerator. The landlord wanted the place, of course, but she couldn't bear to go through her mother's belongings yet; she couldn't even bear to think about it.

"I'm afraid there's not much room," she said.

"I don't own much stuff," I said. I'd rented a small room for my drawing table in a suite occupied by a faltering film-distribution company, so I didn't even have my work to carry around

"Oh," she said, finishing off her wine with a great swallow. "This is a much nicer place than where I live with my husband."

"Why don't you move here then?" I asked.

"Because we barely fit into the twenty-two hundred square feet of space we have now," she said. She got up, lifted her empty glass at me, and said, "Just tell me when you want more."

She left me calculating how many of these apartments could fit into twenty-two hundred square feet: five, I decided, maybe six.

"I don't even remember my father, I was so young when he died," said Debby from the kitchen. She hadn't actually used the word "died" about her mother, but my friend Dee Kilmartin had filled me in the night before, on the phone. Dee had heard about the apartment from her assistant, who had told her it really had to go to someone Debby could trust.

When Debby got back into her seat with a new glass of wine, she twisted around and hooked her left leg over an arm of the chair. "Are your parents still alive?" she asked, and then she added, "I would never sit like this anywhere else."

"They live in Massachusetts," I said, and she nodded.

She had such a fetching face, with her big blue eyes and full, pouty mouth. At the same time, she looked as if someone had borne down on her while she was trying to grow up: she was short and sturdy and a little wide, without much of a waist or neck and with slightly bowed legs.

I was more interested in her clothes than her looks, however, because Dee had told me that Debby was a buyer at a department store. She was wearing mustard and chartreuse and a kind of cinnamon—new colors that as far as I could tell only the very young had taken up. For a moment my black dress made me feel old, which I suppose I was, compared to Debby. Even those muddy colors couldn't sour her rosy complexion; her curly black hair shone like a reflection in a pond (mine I was already dyeing); and her sturdy little body was so unmarked it could have just come out of the kiln.

"I thought of going off on my own like that," said Debby. "There's something incredibly appealing about it. But I couldn't come to New York, because I'm already here, and where else is there to go? Besides, families can be useful. What if you get arrested for something you didn't do, and you need someone to post bail?"

I said, "I have a couple of friends who'd post bail even if I were guilty."

"Well, I wouldn't be guilty," said Debby. She may have been apologizing. "I got married right after I graduated from college," she added.

"Oh, yes?" I said.

"Alan was the first person I went out with who wasn't at least ten years older than I was."

I nodded, and she said, "He's a doctor, though," and got herself a third glass of wine. Then she asked if she could come by to look through her mother's things sometime, and when I said yes, she cried, "What size are your feet? I can give you some of her shoes!"

I didn't know what to say. Did this mean she thought I wore the same styles as her mother?

"My mother loved shoes," said Debby. "She bought fourteen pairs in one day when she had her nervous breakdown."

"That's a lot of shoes," I said.

"She used to be a pianist, but then she had her nervous breakdown and became a guidance counselor."

It's hard to describe the tone she used. Some combination of shame and defiance is what you'd expect, but Debby spoke with—well, satisfaction is probably the best word. It was as if she were speaking of something she could count on, and so didn't value much, like the punctuality of a certain friend, or a sense of rhythm. She used the same tone when she told me her mother took the apartment because it was so small she could never change her mind and get another piano. I looked at the place differently after that: the size became both a comfort (no hulking, threatening pianos here, thank you) and a thrill (what an escape!).

When we finally discussed money, Debby was as straightforward about that as about everything else. I never told her I was going to take the place; I guess it didn't occur to either of us that I might not.

I'd never before had a sublet like it. The best way to illustrate this is to say that two of the dozen or so places I'd taken in the past had once been rented by rock critics. This was coincidence, in a way, but it was a coincidence that made sense: the sort of marginal areas where rock critics could start plying their trade in the early seventies had since become so expensive that people refused to give up their leases. On the other hand, these people still didn't have the money to let the places sit idle while they were away. If they did, they'd move, to someplace where the plaster wasn't cracked and the stairs didn't lean.

Also, most sublets—like most apartments—show such safe good taste that everything is beige or kitsch. Here, there was a pink chair, a blue chair, a lavender-splashed couch. There was a portrait of Debby as a little girl looking at an Airedale. There was a china plate in metal clasps on the wall; there were some fake ferns; there were those dust ruffles. It was too . . . *personal.* Worse, the place was not prepared for me. A sublet may be full of a person's possessions, but generally the brush and comb, the shower cap, the reading glasses, are packed away; the medicine cabinet is picked over; the secrets are stashed in boxes at the back of a drawer. Here there were two paperback romances on the night table, one with a cat-shaped bookmark still stuck in it. I opened it up and read, "Janine was afraid she was becoming fussy and old-maidish."

I took these books and the other things from the surfaces I thought I'd be using every day and put them in a video-store bag I'd used to supplement my one suitcase. Later, I crowded all of Debby's mother's food over to the right side of the refrigerator, so I could fit some of my own in. I used a dab of her ketchup on a hot dog.

Debby eventually showed up again, but before she did, I took my new love Anthony to a bar near a sublet I'd shared with a poet almost eight years ago. (When you've never had an apartment of your own, the restaurants and bars you frequent become incredibly important.) Anthony and I were on the Lower East Side anyway, because of a May Day celebration for some Russian émigré artist, so I insisted we stop and have a drink, just the two of us.

When I'd lived nearby—in a perpetually chilly basement with whitewashed stone walls—I'd been about Debby's age, and I suppose that's why I wanted to see the place again. I had already told Anthony all about her

—about the apartment and the wine and the offer of her mother's shoes and the way she had referred to her mother's nervous breakdown—so I said only, "If I'd gotten married as young as Debby did, I'd never have met you."

"My life would have been ruined," said Anthony. He was in a good mood, having just figured out how to apply chaos theory to yet another innocent phenomenon.

"Plus I wouldn't have lived in so many places," I said. "I would never have met Curtis or Tina or Jane S., because I met them all through this one guy, what's-his-name, Mr. Operetta. I wouldn't have gone to Phoenix with Vernon Westbay."

"I thought you got robbed in Phoenix."

"I wouldn't have gotten robbed," I said. "I wouldn't know how to slip money to a super. I wouldn't know how to look so mean people leave you alone on the street. I wouldn't know how to make a couple of dollars last till Tuesday."

Our shots came, I paid from a fan of bills on the pockmarked table, and Anthony said, "Take the mother's shoes. It'll make the kid feel better. At least the shoes will be living on."

I basically believe everything Anthony says, so when Debby showed up at the apartment that Saturday, carrying a bottle of wine, I tried to look interested and helpful. There were no closets—the place was too old for them—but in the bedroom was a huge old wooden cupboard with a full-length mirror that Debby exposed when she opened one door. We looked at ourselves together, then looked away.

"Haven't you had a chance to move in?" said Debby suddenly.

"I'm moved in," I said.

"Oh," she said. "I hadn't noticed any of your things."

I sat on the bed near her as she started to pull shoes off shoe trees, but it turned out that Mrs. Bresselman had had much smaller feet than anyone either Debby or I knew, so Debby filled three large shopping bags for the Salvation Army. She crawled farther back into the cupboard. "Oh, God," she cried, "I didn't know she still had these. Remember when the boots all laced up, and the skirts buttoned down the front?" She emerged displaying a pair of boots that looked remarkably like the ones I was so proud of when I went off to college. Debby said, "I could swear she wore these my first day of school." It was amazing to think an adult could be so much younger than I was.

I said, "I still remember the plaid lunch box I took to my first day of school. If people knew how often these things were going to reappear in nightmares, they'd choose them more carefully."

"I liked school," she said, unhooking a few hangers and throwing clothes on the bed. And when I didn't reply, she said, "I would love to be as independent as you."

"What gives you the impression I'm independent?" I

asked, and she said, "Well, you're not exactly weighted down with worldly possessions, are you?"

She thrust a lilac-colored skirt at me. "Go try this on," she said.

It's not like she expected me to strip right there in front of her, but it's still embarrassing to try on clothes for people you don't know. You can't tell what you might look like. I was game, though. I went into the living room and pulled on the skirt, which fortunately didn't meet at the waist. I could see why Debby wasn't bothering to try on these things herself.

"It doesn't fit," I called out. The door to the bedroom opened immediately, and there she was again, only a foot away, with more clothes.

"That was always small on her, too," she said, holding the hangers to her chest with one hand and tugging at my right side with the other. "She never buttoned it, either." I stepped back. "Try these," she said, following me. She threw the clothes on the couch with a clatter.

These were not at all like fresh new clothes in a store, you understand. Anything can happen in clothes like that. These clothes were decidedly someone else's, worn in spots and still conforming to an alien shape.

"Try this first," said Debby, holding a suit jacket up against my back to gauge the fit. "You should wear it with red. My mother always did. See, there's a little red in the weave here, almost a burgundy." And when I had put the suit on—it was very loosely constructed and so fit, sort of—she cried, "Look at all that leg!"

I looked down, and she said, "I guess you're taller than she was."

"I guess so," I said.

"We could have taken care of her for years, you know. We have the money."

I nodded. For a moment I was afraid she was going to cry, but she started picking through clothes again. I wondered how many I was going to have to try on.

"I got married three weeks after I graduated from college," she said. "Three weeks to the day."

"You told me," I said.

"At least I've never been lonely," she said, which started me thinking that maybe she was.

"You get a better deal on an apartment when you're part of a couple," I said.

Debby got herself some wine and lay back on the couch against some dresses, so relaxed that her head was tilted back at what looked like a throat-crushing angle. She said, "Once when I was still living here, I came home and there was someone in the kitchen, a friend of my mother's. He'd jimmied the lock. He was just standing there, looking at the clock, probably thinking about time. He used to teach philosophy at the Sorbonne, and he was so smart, it made him crazy. He's a diagnosed schizophrenic."

I tried on a lot of clothes that day. I remember a white silk shirt ("My mother always wore the cuffs turned back," said Debby, so I turned them back), a flowered cotton shirt with two buttons missing ("She was always so lazy," said Debby in that strangely satisfied tone of hers), a short black circle skirt that made me look like a figure skater, and a black cotton cardigan ("Just take it," said Debby, "she never wore it," as if for that reason there was no need to try it on). In the end, I accepted nearly everything Debby offered me and put it all back in the cupboard where it had come from.

When Anthony called that night, I insisted on meeting him twenty blocks out of our way, at the Horse Bar. I find it very comforting, in part because of the decor, which has never changed: pictures of racehorses are nailed to the cheap paneling in each of the booths. I sat under Affirmed. While I ate a sliced-steak sandwich, another couple showed up and told us stories about a painter we all knew who used real fur in his work. Then I told them about Debby. I didn't know the point of the story when I started telling it, but by the end, everybody was laughing.

In some ways my life varies according to what sort of apartment I've sublet. Once I stayed in a place off lower Fifth Avenue that had a real dining room and a chandelier on a dimmer and a funny old oak table and a set of open shelves full of china and stemware. I gave a lot of dinner parties there. Another place, owned by an Indian dancer, had a little Shiva shrine and a big claw bathtub and not much else—the bed was as hard and skinny as a ski—so I would read in the tub, occasionally turning on the hot-water tap with my toes. Or sometimes I'd just lie there, keenly feeling the line on my skin where warm water became cooler air. I did a lot of daydreaming those few months. In one apartment I spent practically no time on the phone, because it was hung on a wall in the kitchen, where there wasn't any place to sit.

But no sublet had as great an impact as this one, because this one was animated. For the next few days, Debby was here and there and everywhere, sorting, stacking; and the more time she spent, the more room everything took up. Released from drawers and boxes, fabric expanded; paper resettled in larger and more awkward clumps. Debby kept giving me clothes and scarves and books mostly photography books, if I remember correctly—but I lost track of which things were for me and which were lying around for some other reason. The refrigerator was full of half bottles of wine. I spent the second weekend at Anthony's, thankful for his double bed, and when I came back, all the plants had disappeared, and the box of towels by the table had turned into a box of bookends, change purses, and extension cords. It was as if the apartment had done stuff on its own while I was away.

The next time Debby came over, she didn't bother to put the wine back in the refrigerator between drinks. "I've had the most fabulous idea," she said, clenching her fists momentarily, as if in the middle of a cheer. "I'm going to get you this lease. I just haven't worked out how to do it."

I didn't know what to say. It was eight o'clock; I'd

been working like a maniac all day and couldn't think. I certainly didn't want to really live there. What sort of future would that be?

"You could pretend to be me," she said, "and sign my name and everything. I wouldn't mind."

I murmured something.

"The landlord has never met me, and you look really young."

"Mmm," I said.

"We'll think of something," she said, opening the wine and leaning back in the couch. "How would Anthony react?" And when I said I wasn't sure, she said, "I'd love to meet him."

"He works a lot," I said.

"Tell me about it," said Debby. "Don't you ever get scared, living alone?" I noticed then that she wasn't looking at all the stuff left to pack, as she usually did. She was looking straight at me, but as if I were a great distance away. It shook me, that look, because I remember giving it to older people once upon a time. I'd be thinking how different from them I was going to be when I was their age: I'd be richer, or more accomplished, or more comfortable, or more loved.

"Every time Alan goes away, there are things about to jump at me from the shadows," she said.

"I have a friend who has to turn off the TV as soon as any scary music comes on," I said. "It all depends on what you're used to."

"I'm going to tell you something I haven't told anybody," she said. "But first don't you want some wine?"

I got myself a glass.

Then she told me about drinking alone—twice—at a seedy bar with a handicappers' special advertised in the window. The bar was not the Horse Bar, but sounded a lot like it. "If you're going to have a drink by yourself, it's better to do it in a place like that," said Debby, "where people assume you're an alcoholic. If you do it at some normal place, people assume you're there to pick someone up."

I nodded.

"That's something my mother's friend Sophie told me, but then, she really was an alcoholic. She was one of the first women on the Stock Exchange."

It occurred to me then that Debby thought I was like these bizarre characters she so enjoyed talking about, and she'd been trying to impress me with them. Over the next few weeks, as she gradually finished cleaning out the apartment, she told me about another pianist who'd declared he was Satan one afternoon and convinced half his students before he was put away, a guy who'd jumped from an observation deck and lived, a couple of relatives who'd disappeared, and an old dancer who'd showed up for dinner one night with nothing on under her ankle-length mink coat.

One Friday in the middle of the summer, a letter addressed to Ms. Deborah Bresselman was waiting in the mailbox when I got home from work. It was from the landlord, and for some reason the stamp hadn't been canceled, which made it look all the more alarming. "Open it up!" cried Debby when I called. "No, don't. I'll be right over. No, I can't! I won't be able to get back in time. Oh, I knew this would happen."

I could hear some kind of soft music in the background—strings, I think—and it gave me a sudden sharp desire to see where Debby lived. Since Anthony wouldn't be coming over until much later, I said I'd take the letter to her, and Debby said, "You deserve that lease."

It took me almost an hour to get there, because I walked most of the way. Debby's apartment was in one of four glass towers that hung out over the river east of Gramercy Park, on the far side of the FDR Drive. The towers were part of a complex with its own pedestrian bridge, its own dry cleaners, its own playground, its own bank. It looked like one of the many hospitals in the area, neither old nor new. Two security guards were strolling toward each other in the middle of the plaza.

Debby greeted me in a small square foyer through which I could see a bit of the living room: the back of a beige couch with two matching beige heads sticking above it, napless wall-to-wall carpeting, a large framed poster of three blue stripes and a pink, a Parsons table of blond wood. The place was nothing like Debby's mother's apartment.

"Is the person who showed up naked under her coat here?" I asked in a low voice.

Debby cut off a little shriek by covering her mouth with one hand.

"How about the person who thinks about time?"

But by then we'd attracted the attention of the others. The two women sitting on the couch had twisted around to look at me, each letting a pale arm dangle down the thickly woven pale upholstery. Two men beyond them had stood up and moved in closer to get a better look, each carrying a wineglass, and another short handsome guy in a blue piqué T-shirt had come around the couch and was walking toward me. They were all younger than I was.

"This is my husband," said Debby.

The living room was huge: walking into it was like walking out of a subway entrance. Everyone continued to stare at me with the same intense interest. "This is Rosemary," said Debby. She sounded proud she knew me.

"We've certainly heard a lot about you," said her husband, clasping my hand, and one of the other men said, "Is it true you've lived out of a suitcase for more than a decade?"

Debby took the letter from me and left the room.

"But she's so stylishly dressed," said one of the women, and the other said, "How do you do it?"

Without waiting for me to answer, this second woman said to the first, "I saw a movie last weekend about a girl who has to pick up a different man every night just to have a place to sleep."

So that was it. *I* was the one who showed up naked under her coat.

"We were originally a nomadic people, you know," said one of the men, sitting down.

"Speak for yourself, Barry." They were all resettling themselves now.

"I'm referring to the whole human race, lamebrain."

"It's why people get restless in the spring. They're supposed to be moving on to greener pastures."

"I get restless every four years, as if I expected to graduate again."

"I'm not making this up. Anthropologists discovered it by studying primitive people."

They went silent when Debby returned and showed me the letter. It said that an unidentified woman with brown hair had been living illegally at the address specified above, which was grounds for eviction. Debby clasped my arm above the elbow. She said, "I'm going to call a lawyer."

"I have to go," I said.

Something woke me up. In front of me was a square of restless blue: the top half of the window. Then I heard a distant "Rosemary!" It was Debby's voice. Anthony tried to pull himself straight beside me in the twin bed.

"It's Debby," I said. It was all I had the chance to say

before she was in the room with us. "Why, Debby," I said.

"I thought I'd drop by to see how you're holding up," she said. "Don't mind me. Alan says I'm pathologically intimate." She sat down on the other bed, which was still made. "You must be Anthony," she said.

"Yes," he said. I had a sleeveless T-shirt on, but he looked as if he were naked under the sheet. He was already furious, I could tell.

"Rosemary has become a real friend of mine," she said. "I suppose you've heard about the letter I got yesterday." She leaned forward. "Do you sublet places, too?"

"No," he said.

"I prefer a more settled life, myself," she said, and added, pointedly looking around, "I hope your place is a little bigger."

This Anthony didn't have to answer, so he didn't. I found myself wondering what Debby thought of him. He's a bit scary-looking, with his narrow foxy features and his sharp eyeteeth. There are people who might believe him if he said he was Satan.

"It's funny to see someone else in my mother's bed," said Debby. "You're a physicist, right? That must pay pretty well, huh?"

She thought she was protecting me, of course, but I didn't mind as much as I should have. She was still so young; she had only the vaguest notion of what people had to be protected against. And with Anthony half twisted above me, half jammed into my back, and Debby unconsciously creeping ever closer on the other bed, I was wedged in as snugly—and agreeably—as if this were not some stranger's bed, in a stranger's apartment, but was the place I was supposed to be.

MY DARLING STRANGER

I had pretty much lost interest in Susannah and
Harry Tierney until my boyfriend Anthony met them for
the first time. This was at the beginning of the summer
last year, and the Tierneys had come down from Connecticut to go to dinner at Dee Kilmartin's. Dee served a
salmon she'd caught somewhere on the Gaspé Peninsula.
There was just the right number of people for the
salmon, but perhaps too many people for a dinner party
—we had to eat in the living room, balancing our plates
on our knees, and it made the atmosphere a bit slap-
happy. Susannah, who was wearing an oversize man's
dress shirt, talked straight through the main course about
her early sex life. This is the sort of thing that a person
as beautiful as she is can get away with. Her dark, nearly
waist-length hair kept falling over her shoulders, and it

struck me that those two wavy tresses, one on either side of her, made her look like a painting of Eve.

"I didn't *lose* my virginity," she said at one point. "I made an appointment to get rid of it. I called up someone I thought would be good at it, and we did it in his father's study. The kid ended up repairing Hammond organs, interestingly enough."

I had heard this before, of course. Friends of Susannah's knew more such details about her life than about their own, which they weren't reminded of constantly. But I was still surprised at Harry's reaction. Harry, when he'd first married Susannah, seemed to be such a dull, eager sort—too perfect a victim for her. He would have suffered agonies during these revelations back then, or made wild, defensive remarks. Now he wasn't bothered at all. Instead he looked a little impatient, as if he wanted to help move some heavy furniture while he had a few spare minutes. He'd become very successful as a lawyer, but I think Susannah was another big reason that he'd come to life this way. It would be hard to be embarrassed or stiff about anything once you were accustomed to her. And Susannah, too, was different. Oh, she was still loud, forward, awkward, engaging. But she used to get herself into terrible states sometimes—there could be a desperate edge to these confidences of hers—and I hadn't seen anything like that since her wedding.

There were largely couples at that dinner. Dee herself was alone, but all kinds of other people had gotten married, people you'd never expect. Liz Quirk had married a community organizer when he'd agreed to maintain a separate residence. Evidently the two of them could attend the same dinner parties, because they were both there. Tina Fleck, who used to retreat into horrified silence when anyone disagreed with her, was there with her husband, and I swear she looked as if her bones had gotten stronger. He was ten years younger than she was, which is probably why the marriage had worked out so well. Susannah was the only woman who'd changed her name. I don't think any of the guests were divorced. In fact, no one whose wedding I'd attended had split up—at least not yet. One couple from Virginia had separated for a month or two, but in the end nothing came of it.

I had been a little nervous about introducing Anthony to so many married people, but I shouldn't have been. I found I didn't care so much what strangers thought, and I hadn't met a lot of the spouses. Susannah hadn't either, of course, so she at least pretended to address one or two of them. By dessert she was onto how she'd gotten the heart tattoo on her right thigh, and her new audience was still enthralled. Even Anthony, who is oddly proper in some ways, couldn't keep his eyes off her. But I could play these stories back in my head so easily that I had almost stopped listening when Susannah suddenly veered to the present and complained that Harry worked too much. "I haven't seen him naked since Wednesday," she said.

"Thursday," said Harry.

"Why should you remember?" said Susannah. "You can see yourself naked any time you like."

"It was still Thursday," said Harry, and Susannah said, "Wednesday. It was the day of my hair appointment."

"That was Thursday," said Harry. "But you might be using a different calendar from the rest of us."

Harry, who had gotten more attractive rather than less over the years, was sitting on Dee's heavily padded teal-blue couch, his legs crossed and one arm slung carelessly over the back. I had a brief wild vision of him in the exact same posture, but with no clothes on. It was a shock. You tend not to think of lawyers that way, as if the sublimating they do were a complete process and they had no bodies left at all. I noticed that a number of guests were staring at Harry with new interest.

"It was as if she were putting him up for bid," said Anthony later, but he's a physicist and is used to theories that have nothing to do with life as we know it.

"She always was a lot of fun," I said vaguely, and Anthony said, "It's lucky the food was so good. It gave the other guests something to do."

After that evening I started asking about the Tierneys again, and every once in a while someone would tell me they weren't getting along. Dee said that Susannah had soaked all the labels off Harry's new wine collection in retaliation for a slighting remark he'd made about her palate. When I repeated this to Anthony, he thought it was so funny—especially the "new" part—that I said suddenly, "Let's meet them for dinner."

Anthony was surprised at first and said something about hiding the knives, but he went along with the idea, and Susannah seemed pleased to hear from me. We agreed to meet at a Thai restaurant where a gangland shooting had taken place six months before.

When the Tierneys arrived, Susannah apologized for being late and said, "Is it my imagination or did Harry leave me waiting at the altar for forty-five minutes?"

Anthony and I had been drinking for long enough that we just laughed. Then Harry said, "Someone in this family has to work," and a silence fell.

Susannah had pretty much stopped doing free-lance design, I'm not sure why. I'd never pressed her because I'd always assumed it was a sore subject. Susannah was not the sort to crumple, however. She said, "It wouldn't matter if he had to support me or not. It's in his nature to work like that. He has a very pale soul. You know what I'm talking about?" This last was addressed to me.

I murmured something.

"Rosemary knows what I mean," Susannah said to Harry.

Then she turned back to me and said, "I want you to listen to this, because it is unbelievable. He didn't make me wait tonight because he had to work; he made me wait because he had to compliment his boss on his tennis game."

"He's not my boss," Harry said to Anthony. "And there's no way she could have known what we were talking about."

"Oh?" said Susannah. "It was his grasp of the English language instead?"

"Susannah, we were on deadline."

"Since Harry never gives a straight answer, fights with him never have to end," Susannah said to me.

This was less fun than hearing about wine labels, and the table seemed awfully small. I don't know how the restaurant could have expected four people to sit at it.

Toward the end of the evening, Susannah said, "Look, no ring." She displayed her hand, fingers spread, as if to catch herself when she fell. "If the fight is big enough, I throw my wedding ring out the window. This was my fifth."

About two weeks later, I found myself with an extra ticket to the musical *My Darling Stranger*—Anthony naturally had to work at the last minute—so I called up Susannah and offered it to her. Ordinarily I would have gone alone rather than ask a married person, but I figured Susannah might need the break. As it turned out, she wanted to see the show as much as I did. *My Darling Stranger* had been playing on Broadway for a couple of years by then, and everyone had something nice to say about it. It was set in New Orleans, a place Susannah had always wanted to visit. And we'd both already heard snatches of the music—part Dixieland and part zydeco —so we knew we'd like at least that much.

It was a Thursday night. Everything was as usual. The gray-haired lady who gave us our programs looked like she belonged in the lingerie section of a department store. The walls were ivory-colored, with raised panels edged in gold. I didn't see too many empty seats. Understudies had stepped in for two of the smaller roles.

The plot, basically, was this: our heroine, an actress, goes to New Orleans on tour, and a man on the street accosts her. He says she used to be his lover, but a rival put a spell on her so that she would forget him. When she tries to shake him off, he follows her to her hotel in the French Quarter, and various misadventures ensue. She resists him and resists him, but finally, when she sees him at a voodoo ceremony, she realizes she's in love. The next day she does the only thing she thinks she can: she pretends to believe his story. She falls into his arms, and the curtain drops.

Intermission came after the hotel scene. Susannah stayed in her chair, waving me out. This didn't surprise me, since it can be boring to mill around once you've quit smoking, but she didn't talk afterward either, not as we put on our coats, not as we stood waiting for the aisle to clear, not as we picked our way down the stairs, not as we burst into the throng on the street, not as the crowd pushed us into the parked cars lining the sidewalk—and at this point I was saying, "What do you want to do? Shall we go get a drink?"

Susannah plunged off down the sidewalk. Her face is ordinarily tilted up and to the right, like a majorette's, but now it was in shadow, and her long dark hair looked like it was about to be zipped closed. Halfway down the block, she turned this dark face to me and said, "Do you think she was really under a spell?"

I said, "No."

"You can't be sure, though," said Susannah. "You really can't be sure."

At the bar with the big wooden parrots hanging from the ceiling, Susannah tripped over a chair by the door and caught the arm of a man who immediately tried to buy her a drink. She ignored him. She said, "Just because she's pretending to believe him doesn't mean that what she's pretending to believe isn't true."

"It's only a musical," I said. Susannah was not usually so interested in imaginary situations.

"I know *you* would never pretend to believe a person like that," said Susannah. "You're too matter-of-fact."

"I suppose," I said.

"But you're not married yet, either," she said. "Before you get married, you expect everything to make sense eventually, and then afterward you see that it never will."

This sounded promising, but I couldn't get anything else out of her. She has never been able to explain herself. But she's also never calculating, never even discreet, so I could be blunt. I asked, "What's going on between you and Harry?" and she said, "The usual." She was also easily bored.

Two days later she called me around noon and said, "The night we saw *My Darling Stranger* together, did the audience laugh when she said she was going to believe him?"

My Darling Stranger

I was late with a cover I was designing for a mystery reference book (I'd decided to read the whole thing first, all the way from *accessory* to *"The Zero Clue"*), so I wasn't really paying attention when I said, "I don't remember anything like that."

"I don't think they did," said Susannah. "And I'm sure they didn't clap when she hid from him at the hotel."

This caught my notice. "You remember a lot more than I do," I said.

"I saw it again," said Susannah. "I brought Fern."

"You went two nights in a row?" I cried. I was . . . I was jealous for some reason.

"That's nothing," said Susannah. "Tonight I'm going with Harry."

In seven months, Susannah saw *My Darling Stranger* sixteen times. After the first few times, I took to saying, "It's my fault. I was the one who started her on this," but of course I was secretly flattered. It made me think more fondly of her, and when Anthony said that if he were Harry, he'd be awfully nervous about this infatuation, I told him not to be ridiculous. Then I called up Susannah and asked her if she wanted to go out for a drink.

We met at the end of the summer, after the sixth time she'd seen the show—a Wednesday matinee—and although her face was not as dark and closed as it had been after the first time, she had obviously been brooding. We were seated at a mullioned window, in a wooden niche facing the street, and outside a bus was filling with ladies in hats who'd also seen the play. They chatted as unselfconsciously as people on TV with the sound turned off. They did not look troubled by art. "You probably think of me as very worldly," said Susannah.

I murmured a vague assent.

"That's where you're wrong," she said. "In some ways I am hopelessly naïve."

"Oh?" I said.

"I'm not, you know, Byzantine. I don't think that way." She looked at me hopefully.

"I see," I said.

"I'm not like the play, I mean," she said. "But that's the way things really are, isn't it?"

"You mean love is based on lies?" I said.

Susannah shook her head, but I got the impression that this was more in perplexity than in disagreement. "Maybe you're supposed to lie to yourself a little," she said, and I said, "She didn't lie to herself, only to him."

"But how can you tell if you're lying to yourself?" she cried. "Hook yourself up to a lie detector?"

My laugh died out when Susannah's face didn't change. She said, "If you love a person one minute and hate him the next, how can both feelings be true?"

"Harry can be such a jerk," I said.

"At least he liked the play," said Susannah. "In the beginning I could barely talk to people who hadn't seen it." Harry had given her the original cast recording and later bought her headphones to go with it. "Maybe I should become an actress," she continued, as if the thought had never occurred to her before. "I'd like to go on tour right now."

My friend Cole told me maybe a month later that the Tierneys had had drinks with him and Steve—Cole was in a couple now, too—and Susannah and Harry had gotten into a fight about whether she should go to the play for the tenth or whatever time it was or whether she should go to Harry's sister's birthday party in New Jersey. "Their fights are so scary to watch," said Cole, and when I agreed, he said, "It's probably just because they're so public." We were more amusing when we got off on a tangent about the unfair techniques used by our own lovers: silence, feigned objectivity, reexamination of long-forgiven sins, unflattering comparisons to much-loved or much-hated parents. "Once Steve asked his twin brother over to talk to me about my 'problems,'" said Cole, and I said, "Once Anthony called me a slug."

Cole and Steve had just moved in together at the time, and I was looking for a sublet big enough for Anthony and me. I almost took a five-room first-floor apartment near a new club, but at the last minute I realized I was long past the age when I'd think the noise was fun. I settled for a one-bedroom in Chelsea that had a real eat-in kitchen. Anthony brought over some clothes and made me watch him hang his shirts in the closet. He rented a machine to clean the living-room rug. He bought a new halogen lamp to stand over his side of the bed. He slept there every night, but he continued to go to his old place every evening when he left the lab, and

soon it became clear that he planned to do so indefi-
nitely. "I have to get my mail," he said, and when I
pointed out that the Post Office forwarded mail to more
difficult places than Twenty-third Street, he said, "Many
things are true in general that are not true for me."

Susannah and I talked about going to the play again
together, but I was in no hurry, and she eventually let
the subject drop. She was very possessive, as if *My Darling Stranger* were a new lover she wanted to keep under
wraps. After a while, she stopped calling at all, but I
heard that she went to the show a thirteenth time, a
fourteenth time, a fifteenth time. She once tried going in
for free after the end of the first act, but she didn't like it.
"I'm getting too old to do without the foreplay," she told
Tina. "And Harry can afford it."

She usually got a single seat, which didn't sound much
like her, but she must have been going around more and
more by herself. She was alone when she met Dotty
Coombs and her husband for dinner on Fifty-seventh
Street, and she wouldn't even let them talk. Apparently
the person who played the hotel clerk in *My Darling
Stranger* was sitting next to them. Neither Dotty nor her
husband recognized him, because his part was so small.
But Susannah kept shutting them up until after the guy
was gone, which was halfway through their meal.

Dee Kilmartin invited Anthony and me to dinner after
the New Year, saying it would be only the three of us
and Harry and Susannah. At first Anthony didn't want to

go. He said, "I don't need to hear some crank go on about some play she thinks she's in." But I told him he had certain responsibilities to me now, and I pinched him and poked him and tickled him until he gave in.

Dee served osso buco, which I'd never had before. Because there were only five of us, we got to sit in the dining room, beside a steamed-up window with a weighted blue curtain at each side. Susannah, who was wrapped in a heavy black cardigan, looked hot and tired. She said little. It was as if all the emotion had left her face, though her eyes glittered a bit feverishly. When I tried to ask her about what she'd been doing lately, she said, "Harry won't let me talk about it."

Harry gave her a look and kept eating.

I said, "Maybe after dinner the men can adjourn to the other room, while the women drink brandy," and Susannah said, "The play has only made my life worth living again."

The radiator clanked and hissed.

"I hate that noise," said Dee.

"That's not hatred," said Susannah. "Only men and women can really hate each other."

I was already looking at my plate, but Dee said, "No, the only people you can really hate are people you're afraid you might be like." She sounded as if she'd been thinking about the subject. She said she hated a former classmate who spent her days choosing the right tea, the right cheese, the right hand-dipped chocolates. Then Anthony said you could hate only people who weren't like you at all, because then you couldn't understand why they did what they did. He hated the old man who lived above us because he was always trying to intrigue with us against the other tenants. I said that you could hate only people you owed something to, but before I could give any of the many examples that came to mind, Dee asked Susannah, "So who do you hate?"

When she didn't answer right away—when she put her hand to her mouth as if to indicate she was still eating, which she wasn't—when she shook her head as if to deny what she was thinking—I was afraid she was going to say, "Harry."

And I wasn't the only one who got that impression. Dee suddenly cried, "How did we get on this awful subject, anyway?" and soon everyone was standing up and looking for coats and saying good-bye.

Then I saw an ad in the paper for the last four performances of *My Darling Stranger*. I called up Susannah and left a message on her machine. When she didn't call back in a week, I called and left another. After a couple of days, I left another. I heard nothing.

I learned that Susannah had gone to New Orleans when I got a postcard of some crumbling old cemetery vaults. On the back she'd written, *I haven't found the hotel yet, but the rest is here: jazz, voodoo, mysterious strangers. I might stay forever.*

It was February, a bleak month in New York. Even our apartment building's entryway, where I read the postcard, was so cold that the air was like a hard, dry pinch on my nose and fingers. Upstairs, I threw my coat on the couch, started to run a hot bath, and dialed Susannah's number again. When the machine answered, I hung up.

I was out of the bath and sitting on the couch reading the paper by the time Anthony came home. I told him about the postcard and said, "You'd think they'd change the message on their machine."

"You *called?*" he said.

At first I didn't understand his surprise.

"Susannah obviously isn't there," he pointed out.

"I was calling Harry, I guess," I said.

"Why? You want to make sure they've split up?"

He was relaxed; he was amused; and for some reason I wanted to punch him in the face. When I politely asked him what he meant, he said, "You'd love it if Susannah walked off into the sunset alone. You'd think it was romantic."

"So?" I said.

There was a nasty silence.

"You're no better," I said. "The only reason you don't want to see Susannah walking off into the sunset alone is that you don't like her much."

"I never said I didn't like Susannah."

"You make it very clear nonetheless." I had started walking up and down the room, making a scything motion with my right hand. "You like *Harry* better," I said in disbelief.

"They're both creeps," said Anthony. "But that's not

what we're talking about." He has this way of brushing his face with his fingers when he gets angry that is the most hateful thing I have ever seen.

"What did you call my friends?" I said.

"Creeps."

I whirled around.

"Maybe that's why you have such a creepy interest in them," he added.

"Don't be so prim," I said.

He was the one sitting on the couch now, his back as straight as a nail file. His arms were folded across his chest. "You are one of the most prurient people I have ever met," he said.

"How would you know?" I said. "You haven't the least idea of how complicated people are. I just wonder what you're afraid of."

"I don't have to listen to this," he said, and he started naming everything he saw. "Coffee table. Glass. Chair. Little table." I tried to break in here and failed. "Dog. Book. Lamp. Lampshade." I cannot tell you enough about that voice. "Pillow. Big chair. Jacket. Rug. Bookcase. Bowl." That voice was making my teeth hurt. "Turtle. Book. Book. Picture of book. Wall. Door."

"Get out, get out, get out, get out," I was saying at the end.

"I live here," he said.

"No you don't," I cried. "You never left your old apartment."

"Half the rent doesn't buy much these days, does it?" he said, and I said, "You talk as if you're keeping me."

"Only you would think of that."

"And you have no idea you're doing it," I said, folding my arms to match his. "Your self-deception amazes me."

There was another silence.

"Just tell me one thing," said Anthony. "Tell me why you're so interested in breaking up the Tierneys."

I said, "That way I'll know what to do when our turn comes."

"You want to leave me," he said. "That's what this is all about." There was a dare in his voice, but we both knew suddenly that this was as far as we were going to go.

"I want to be prepared" was all I could say. I was more interested in whether an unlikely black crescent in the carpet was supposed to be there, or whether it was a stain.

It was Anthony who said, "We need a lot more practice arguing then," and pulled me down in his lap.

Into the sudden warmth of his neck I said, "I think we do just fine."

"You have to start talking about your sex life," he said, and I said, "You're going to have to be gone more often."

Somehow, as we checked out arms, legs, lips—to make sure we were both still safe—the glass got knocked off the coffee table, and I said, "Look, we even broke something."

I can't say I was surprised when Susannah called from Connecticut a week after I got her postcard. I wasn't even surprised that she was in a great mood. Anthony was still at the lab, and I had had such a late lunch that dinner was out of the question, so I was stretched out on the bed with a stout and I felt free to talk in the sort of wandering way I hadn't in ages. I gave Susannah a version of the fight her postcard had caused—leaving out the "creeps" part, of course, and implying that I'd been jealous of her supposed flight to freedom, which had in turn annoyed Anthony. I did not tell her that we'd made up, which seemed too intimate a detail, but she assumed it anyway.

She said, "It's weird, the fights you can have and still come out perfectly normal at the other end."

What could I say? I'd come out pretty much the same at the other end, and although I wasn't sure Susannah had, even her marriage was less fragile than I'd assumed. I said, "When I got your postcard I thought for a moment you were leaving Harry."

Susannah laughed. "I hope he can put up with my going to New Orleans a couple more times. It's such a nice place."

I asked her if anyone had accosted her with a wild story about a former love.

"I wish," she said.

"So what did you do?" I asked.

"Mainly I went to the show."

"*My Darling Stranger?*" I asked with surprise, and Susannah said, "Oh, it's been on tour for a while now. It went to New Orleans for Mardi Gras. The production was pretty much the same. The actors were different, of course. And the set seemed a bit smaller. They sold drawing powder in the lobby."

I don't think I'd really wanted Harry and Susannah to break up. There I was, perfectly happy and normal, laid out on the bed: happy boots, happy legs, happy stout. Or, rather, if I felt the tiniest fraction of disappointment, it wasn't enough to interest anyone except for Anthony.

POSSIBILITIES

〰〰〰

$\mathscr{A}$ nthony's old friend Wanda put it this way: "Anthony would say he was thirsty, and Frank would go off and drink a glass of water."

It had started twenty years before, when Anthony and Frank were roommates their freshman year in college. Wanda claimed to have been in the room when they first spoke. She'd come by the dorm with Frank after dinner, and there they found Anthony heating a can of Pioneer brand chili on a hot plate. Anthony held up the can, pointed to the trapper on the label, and said, "Nice jacket, don't you think?" Frank went into town the next day and came back wearing a deerskin jacket just like the one on the can.

Wanda told this as a funny story for a while, but no one much believed her. With her long red hair and thin bluish skin, she must have looked a little more hysterical than anyone she talked about, especially Frank, who was so ordinary. He was from West Hartford; he had shoulder-length brown hair and regular features; his father was in insurance. Frank had even been considered a leader in high school: he had been captain of the track team. Anthony had a certain reserve that many people found attractive. He had also discovered something about the way snowflakes are formed. But he didn't have as many friends as Frank. And if you saw Frank gliding across campus with some fellow runners, say, or a couple of pre-meds and a cutup from Long Island, he seemed as adept as they in the sort of one-upmanship most friendships require.

After Christmas vacation, though, Anthony said he'd always wanted to act, and that week Frank got a small part in a student production of *Julius Caesar.* When Anthony said Calpurnia was pretty, Frank asked her to the movies. When Anthony made fun of sociology, Frank dropped his course in Comparative Deviations. Wanda kept saying to anyone who would listen, "What did I tell you? What did I *tell* you?" At first Anthony seemed flattered. But then one day he announced irritably that he never wanted to know what time it was again, and that night, at dinner, Wanda pointed to a newly exposed circle of white skin on Frank's wrist. Anthony got up and left the table.

Cambodia was bombed that spring, and students everywhere were defying their parents, but when Frank announced he was going to California to pick fruit instead of staying home to work at a law firm, Anthony knew it was because he had just been talking about migrant workers. He stormed about. He called Wanda and raved. That night she ran into Frank over by the playing fields and told him to cut it out. Frank laughed. Then he looked off through the tiers and tiers of spooky wooden seats in the grandstand and said, "Anthony always gives me the idea that there are other ways of doing things."

Wanda chose her words carefully. "We weren't sure you recognized what you were doing," she said.

"Of course I see it," said Frank. He gave her a kiss, which slipped off her lips as she turned away. She had been heading toward the library, but she decided to look for Anthony instead. She found him alone in his room, listening to the radio. An hour later, they made love for the first time.

Frank stopped wearing the deerskin jacket and didn't try out for any more plays; he put on his watch; he found a couple of nice girlfriends. He and Anthony took separate rooms the following year, and they rarely spoke. Anthony discovered something else about snowflakes; Frank became co-captain of the track team. Eventually he applied to law school. But shortly before graduation Anthony told a whole table full of people at a bar that there was nothing more satisfying than working with your hands, and the next thing anyone knew, Frank was back in California, building solar convectors on rooftops. It was two years before he went to law school, and when he got out, he moved to Washington, where he became an energy expert.

Anthony didn't see him again for close to ten years. Wanda, who kept in touch with both of them, wasn't even allowed to mention Frank's name. Anthony was at Cornell for a while, then Rockefeller University, then Los Alamos, then Rockefeller University again. Shortly after he'd moved to New York for the second time, Wanda gave him a call. She was going to marry a guy she'd known for exactly one month—he was a TV producer—and she was going to invite Frank to the wedding. At first Anthony was furious and told her he wouldn't go, but he soon had second thoughts. "When I was really young, crazy people used to scare me" is how he explained himself to me at Wanda's all-white loft one evening. "But later on I got more accepting." He hatched a plot: he would do some good in the world. He read up on energy and told Wanda to put Frank at his table. All through the reception, Anthony talked at him: "Surely you've heard of magnetic levitation," he said, and "We must shut down the nuclear plants while we still have something to leave to our children," and "What ever happened to the electric car?" He also admired the way Wanda waltzed. Frank went home and took dance lessons.

"After that, whenever Frank was in town, I had the two of them over together," said Wanda. "Anthony and I could spend hours speculating on what he would pirate."

I was listening to all this in the dead center of August,

and there was no air-conditioning in Wanda's loft, of course. Her husband—an edgy type who managed to look impatient even in that thick, fish tank–like air—was silently fanning himself with a postcard of a sailboat.

"It was always something he wouldn't ordinarily do in a million years," said Anthony. "At Wanda's first dinner he picked up on how much I admired someone, I forget who, but I know he'd never heard of him."

"It was the fractals guy," said Wanda.

"Physics?" I said.

"Physics," said Wanda. "Later Frank went up to him at a party in Washington and tried to talk to him about predicting stock-market fluctuations."

"As if you could make a killing using chaos theory," said Anthony. "But he doesn't care what he says. He can't be embarrassed."

"Remember when he picked a fight with your landlord?"

Anthony shook his head sadly. "After I'd managed to hold my tongue all those years. But what was most extraordinary was when I'd had such a great time at that conference in Copenhagen, and Frank moved there for a year and a half. It was eerie. I was sure I'd never mentioned the place to him."

"On top of everything else, he's psychic," said Wanda.

"Plus he must have a great job," I said. "If he can take off like that anytime he pleases."

Anthony and Wanda often talked about Frank, and it had begun to bother me. It's not that I minded the fact of

Anthony and Wanda's affair. It had been brief, and it had been a long time ago. Besides, hearing about it was a little like hearing about your parents' childhood: what might have been true back then could not possibly be true in the same sense today. I could not imagine Anthony and Wanda kissing.

But this business with Frank was creepy—all the more so because you could see why Anthony would be the object of such a strange fixation. I had thought him shady-looking at first. Then he'd started to look as if he'd just checked in from somewhere, perhaps one of those in-between dimensions of his. Even at Wanda's, he would fold his long, freckled arms behind his head, and his eyes would go back and forth, back and forth, while people talked around him. Then he'd drop his arms and crane forward over the table to speak, as if he were finally joining us for a quick dip. No one else I know would interest a Frank; no one else I know would encourage one.

I tried to ask Anthony about Frank that night as we were getting ready for bed. I said, "You make fun of this guy, but sometimes I think I hear more about his past than yours."

"Oh, my past," said Anthony, dismissing it with a shrug. "That's all physics." He straightened a pair of shoe trees into his shoes with two dull snaps. I'd never been out with anyone else who used shoe trees.

I said, "I never noticed you having any trouble telling me about certain key triumphs in that field." He didn't respond to this, so I said, "Do you feel responsible for what Frank does?"

"What does it matter?" said Anthony. "It's not like he ends up robbing gas stations." There was a crackle of static as he took off his silky black T-shirt, arms crossed.

"He bothers me," I said.

Anthony always rolls his shirts over and over in his hands to pull them straight before dropping them on the chair. This was what he was doing when he said, "He bothers me, too. It looks like Frank does the things I can only talk about. And it's not true. I don't want to do any of that stuff. Not really."

About a week later Anthony and I decided to get married. He was reading about some physics friends in a physics journal, and I was pretending to write to an old boyfriend in Hong Kong. Anthony looked up and asked me if I thought getting married was a good idea. I said, "Of course I do." We had been drinking stout, but we went out for champagne, so in the end we had Black Velvets in our stomachs.

It seemed forever before we told anyone. Anthony can be almost pathologically private, which is in one way good: he has secrets he has told only to me. I can't think of anything I've told only to him, except maybe what I had for dinner, or what our upstairs neighbor said to our downstairs neighbor. But Anthony's reserve also had its drawbacks. One was that I started to think of a wedding as a shockingly intimate event and, as a result, put off making plans to the last minute.

This was unfortunate, because although I enjoyed learning about halls and dresses—I could imagine a wedding to go with each—I hated it when I had to start making choices. If, say, we had a party in a loft my friend Dee Kilmartin knew about, then I would never steal quietly over the state line, or have a big bash at a hotel with ice sculpted in the shape of diving porpoises. It was heartbreaking to give up either of these possibilities. The only easy decision was to have the wedding itself at a judge's chambers. It was what Anthony wanted, and I had few fantasies about rediscovering religion at this late date. But who to invite there, who to invite later, and what later should be—all of these things were impossible to decide. Should the food be really bad, like at a normal wedding, or should it be only sort of bad?

It was Wanda who brought up Frank. Anthony and I finally told her about our engagement at a bar in a midtown hotel, where the tables were divided from the rest of the huge vaulted space by green velvet ropes. "I knew it!" she cried. She was in a trim gray suit but it didn't seem to rein her in at all. The peplum could have been her jacket leaking. Her red hair stuck this way and that. She asked if she could be the one to call Frank. "I can't wait to see what he does," she said.

Anthony shrugged. Occasionally he seemed encased in a shell of flash and glint—watch face, cuff links, polished shoes—all of which you couldn't quite see past, but this time his face was shining, too. He looked great.

"Aren't you going to invite him?" asked Wanda.

"I hadn't thought about it," said Anthony.

"He'd be so pleased," said Wanda.

"I'm sure he's invited to too many weddings as it is," said Anthony. "He always knew a lot more people than you or I."

"Aren't you curious to see what happens?" said Wanda, looking at me for support, so I said, "I've never even met the guy."

"Weddings are crazy enough," said Anthony, and he told a story I'd already heard about how a sister of a friend of his had married a much older man who already had two daughters around her age. Anthony's friend had slept with one of them after the reception. "He became uncle and lover all in one four-hour period," said Anthony. "When two people get married, everyone comes unhinged."

Wanda had a sudden thought. "You're going to invite me, aren't you?" she said.

"Of course," I said. "We're inviting only people we slept with."

"My God, Rosemary," said Anthony, frowning uncomfortably. And later, when Wanda had left us to pick up her husband at work, he said, "Just don't sleep with Frank. Even after I'm dead."

It was funny that he should have mentioned this. Ordinarily I don't care what I dream, as long as I don't get so scared I wake up. People who talk about their dreams always seem surprised by them, but I never am. Once I slept with my dog, who was named Jasper and who died maybe ten years ago. Another time I slept with a red car, which kind of drove over me. I didn't think twice about it. Still, it was funny that Anthony was worrying about me and someone I didn't even know when I had just started sleeping—in my dreams—with everyone I did know. The night we decided to get married, I slept with a guy named Tom Barbee, who had stupidly left his wife several weeks before. Next I slept with a colleague of Anthony's named Rob. The night before we met Wanda for drinks, I slept with the old boyfriend who lived in Hong Kong. I decided not to tell Anthony any of this.

Because the two of us were teetering on the verge of something too important to think about (I was wearing my solid-gold engagement earrings) and because the bar was so different from our usual ones (no handicappers' specials here), I had a sense that anything might happen before we finished our drinks. At the same time, I knew that this was no longer true.

That night I slept with a man in a white suit I was afraid was Frank but then was much relieved to discover was Anthony's brother, which made it all right; it kept it in the family.

Eventually I agreed to have the reception at the Astronomers' Club, which was a thin slice of a brick building near midtown. Not many astronomers belonged anymore. Anthony's friend Julius, who had been a member for nearly fifty years and who had given up astrophysics for particle physics long ago, claimed you didn't even have to be a scientist to join now. But there were photographs from the *Viking* 2 voyage to Mars in one room, pieces of meteorite in another, and glass cabinets of antique telescopes in a third. Aside from that, it was like any club, with heavy gilt frames and dark velvet sofas and serpentine-legged chairs. There were also several anterooms to wander through, and I liked that. It was expensive, but our parents wanted to help, and I had some savings. Since I'd always lived in sublets, I'd never frittered away money on sheets or plates or a nice little TV. We invited about seventy people, including Frank. On his reply card he wrote, *I can't wait.*

The day we got Frank's card, Anthony bought a black double-breasted silk suit for the wedding. It had a supple shimmer to it and looked as soft as pajamas. Why a person as reserved as Anthony should choose such showy clothes, I don't know; perhaps it was a sort of smoke screen.

"I bet you didn't dress like that when you first met Frank," I said as Anthony admired himself in the mirror tacked to the back of the closet door.

"Of course not," he said. "I wore a pair of dark-green work pants everywhere."

"And a vest," I said. When he didn't respond, I said, "You wore a vest everywhere."

"Not everywhere."

"Then a hat."

This he admitted.

"Who would have thought," I said. I continued to poke and pat his new black suit, but I'd just had a scare—a flash of Anthony at school. Skinny arms, blotter acid, "interesting" hat, long nights at the lab. It's not that I disliked this type when I was at school. I might even have hung out with him. But that he could be seen as a type at all chilled me. It fixed him too much.

"You don't like hats," he said, and I said, "No, no. I like hats. I love hats."

That night I dreamed I slept with Julius, but it was all right because he was so old.

I can't remember all we went through in the last couple of weeks before the wedding. Wanda gave us a dinner; Anthony's parents gave us a dinner; his brother flew in from California and insisted on taking us to a transvestite show near Times Square, which was so packed we had to stand at the bar. My mother took the bus down early from Massachusetts and hung around the apartment a lot, praising everything. She gave a dinner and invited a bunch of relatives, some of whom I'd never met. Dee Kilmartin wanted to throw us a party, but I persuaded her that a ladies' lunch would be a better idea.

She chose a restaurant in Chinatown, where, years before, she and I used to meet for lunch on Fridays. Liz Quirk was there, of course, and so was Eileen Filley and Dotty Coombs and Susannah Tierney. Wanda came late, and if I hadn't known better, I'd have thought she was a bit shy. I forget how many Blue Hawaiis we had. I insisted on ordering shark and jellyfish and other dishes I'd never had before. They weren't very good, so we filled up on drinks. Wanda didn't talk much at first, but she eventually told the story about Frank. Luckily the only person at the table that I'd already told was Liz, who appeared to be interested in hearing it all again.

"He's coming to the wedding?" Wanda asked me.

I nodded.

"Anthony didn't want to invite him at first," Wanda explained to the others.

There seemed to be a pair of cooked antennae on my plate.

"Who'd want to see another person act out whatever happened to cross your mind?" said Wanda. "It could be very embarrassing."

"Like this guy could tell Rosemary he wished she were blond." That was Liz's suggestion.

"Or he could tell her to shut her big mouth." That was Susannah's.

"Or he could surprise me with a nice bottle of perfume." That was mine.

We were sitting at a circular table in the center of a room decorated with panels of multicolored dragons, mouths agape, legs wheeling, tails standing nearly as high as their heads. Ours was the only party left; everyone else had finished and gone. "I can't wait," said Wanda.

At the end Eileen Filley was provoked by the fortune

in her fortune cookie, which read, YOU ARE LUCKY IN LOVE. "Ha!" she said. "I can't remember a romance that lasted more than a weekend."

I could have pointed out that she'd given away at least one great boyfriend, but instead I said, "Maybe that's the luck."

Afterward I regretted this, because it is not the sort of thing that should be said by a woman who is madly in love with her future husband—and I really was. I didn't want to give anyone a different impression.

Anthony showed up as Dee was paying the check. I hadn't expected him. One moment there was a person coming through the door, and the next moment it was Anthony. It's funny how that happens. It's almost as if the shape of the air around a person you like changes as you recognize him. "Anthony!" I cried, and the way Dee and the rest of them scattered, you'd think they'd never seen a man up close before.

As Anthony and I walked up to Canal Street to look at wedding rings, I said, "Wanda told everybody about Frank."

Anthony took a couple of steps through the cold November air. Then he said, "I could call him up and talk about how much I want to go to the Soviet Union."

This did not cheer me up. We walked past two pairs of tourists holding hands. We walked past a Chinese couple standing in the door of their knickknack shop. I said, "I wish you hadn't invited him."

"So do I," said Anthony. "I keep thinking that if I'd

done things differently, I never would have had to meet him."

I used to love Anthony because he made me nervous, because he seemed to alight only momentarily in our conversations, and because my brain hurt when I caught glimpses of where his work went. Now I loved him because I knew him so well. There was something about the way he said, "So do I," about the way he smiled afterward, about the way he continued to walk beside me —vexed, fatalistic, tender.

That night I dreamed I slept with Wanda. I felt a horrible, heavy guilt while I was doing this, but soon I realized that I was not truly being unfaithful, since Wanda was a woman. It was a great relief.

The ceremony started late because we had to wait for Anthony's brother. In fact, the delay was longer than the ceremony itself and gave it a nice fullness. My mother threw rice on the courthouse steps.

I had forgotten all about Frank until Anthony introduced us in the receiving line. I had been vaguely aware of brown hair, medium build, loose grin—yet another person I had nothing to say to—but once I learned this fellow's identity, I looked more closely. He had that stringy, bunched, knotty look that some runners have, and he was slighter than I'd expected, but he just didn't look crazy. He had a baby face, with a snub nose and big black eyes. His hair was short now and combed to one side. The tops of his ears curled away from his head like

handles on a cup. He looked pleasant, enthusiastic, diffident. He said, "I've known your husband a long time."
He stopped, looked at Anthony, and started again. "I've
known your husband for twenty years." Suddenly he
spread his arms and cried, "This is the sexiest wedding
I've ever been to."

Some cousins of Anthony's were next in line. All three
were in identical yellow gowns—bridesmaids' dresses
from another wedding, one of them explained. The oldest one, who was maybe eighteen, said, "Who is that
man?" indicating Frank with her eyes.

"An old friend of Anthony's," I said, and she blushed
She wouldn't say anything more.

When Wanda came through, she was kind of smiling
to herself. She said, "Frank seems to have so much more
to say than usual," and Anthony said—absently, while
shaking her husband's hand—"Oh, really?"

"You'll see," she said.

When Susannah came through, wearing a black
spandex tube dress, she lagged behind her husband a bit
to ask, "Who is that fellow with Tom Barbee's wife?"

There were all sorts of people milling by the door, and
I had to step back and crane my neck, but I picked out
Frank fast enough. "That's the guy Wanda was telling
you about at lunch," I said.

Susannah laughed. She said, "He just told me I had
arms like lilies and legs like a long night of love. Or
maybe it was the other way around."

Anthony blanched and took my hand. "He didn't get it from me," he said. "I swear."

"Where did you get that dress?" The next woman in line was speaking, someone I didn't recognize.

"Look at all those layers," said her friend, lifting one of my overskirts.

The dress was indeed layered, as well as short and pink, and all through the reception people kept coming up to tell me so, or to tell me the things Frank was saying. Dee Kilmartin had hair like silk. Anthony's friend Saundra had a mouth like a strawberry. An older lady in sales had eyes as bright as the sequins on her gold lamé top. I don't know what Eileen Filley had, but it resulted in bitter words on her side. For a while I followed him with my eyes. Around him there was always an extra frisson of energy: someone was leaning forward or recoiling or lifting a hand. At one point I overheard him say to a ten-year-old girl reading a paperback, "That's my favorite book!"

He must have hit on everyone. Fern thought he was making fun of her. Liz Quirk told him to sleep it off. My cousin Sue asked me if she should go to Puerto Rico with him. My mother asked if he was a nice man. None of this seemed to bother any of the husbands or boyfriends. Maybe Frank showed some restraint around them, but I doubt it. His lewdness was purer and less cagey than that. Cole said, "Is he supposed to be straight?" and I said, "I guess so," and he said, "Don't count on it."

At dinner Anthony said, "You know I wasn't thinking

of any of that," but before I could reply, his mother asked if there was any place his brother could lie down. When she'd left, Anthony looked down at his plate and said, "I'm not really hungry."

I never saw Frank eat. He was too busy. When I went to the kitchen to look for aspirin for Anthony's brother, I found Frank chatting with one of the caterers. When there was a line for the ladies' room he was leaning against the wall opposite it. When I went to get a cab for Julius and his wife, I saw Frank lying across a light-blue loveseat in the first anteroom, his head in the lap of Cole's Nigerian friend Frieda, the sweater designer.

"I wouldn't worry about it," said Dotty Coombs, who caught me as I was coming back into the room where the antique telescopes were. "The last wedding I went to, the groom himself came on to me. That was about a year ago, and the marriage is still going strong."

I gave her a quizzical smile, as if I didn't know what she was talking about.

Next it was Wanda, who pretended to be studying a star chart as she told me no one had noticed. She took off before I could say, "Noticed what?"

Then Cole said, "What is this story about Anthony and Frank I've been hearing?"

As he spoke, I could see, on the other side of the room, Anthony stepping back in alarm: Eileen Filley had tried to kiss him on the cheek. He seemed, suddenly, so palpably *there*. It was enough to make a person faint with desire. Anthony saw me watching him then, and in an instant he was beside me, taking my arm and pulling me into the anteroom. He said, "I know I did something wrong, but I can't figure out what it is."

Once upon a time I'd assumed husbands and wives would know everything about each other. By the time Anthony and I decided on a wedding date, I realized this was unrealistic. As the date approached, it didn't even seem polite. But I decided, as we sat there, on the light-blue loveseat where Frank had been lying earlier, to tell Anthony about my dreams. I knew, after all, how scary it was to pick out one person to marry; it was as if you had to pick out only one self to match. And how can you be only one person, when you have the whole world in your head?

As soon as I'd finished, Anthony looked better. He said, "I'm glad you never dreamed you slept with Frank."

And I said, "There's plenty of time yet."

ABOUT THE AUTHOR

JACQUELINE CAREY's stories have appeared in *The New Yorker* and *Wigwag*. She now lives with her husband and daughter in Brooklyn.